parABnormal Magazine

June 2025

Edited by H. David Blalock

parABnormal Magazine
June 2025

All rights reserved. No part of this book may be reproduced or transmitted in any form or by any means, electronic or mechanical, including photocopying or recording or by any information storage and retrieval systems, without expressed written consent of the authors and/or artists.

parABnormal Magazine is a work of fiction. Names, characters, places, and incidents are products of the authors' imaginations. Any resemblance to actual events or persons, living or dead, is entirely coincidental.

Story and illustration copyrights owned by the respective authors and artists.

    Cover illustration by Christina May
    Cover design by Marcia A. Borell
    First Printing, June 2025
    Hiraeth Publishing http://www.hiraethsffh.com/

Vol. VII, No. 2, Issue 26   June 2025

parABnormal Magazine is published quarterly on the 15th day of March, June, September, and December in the United States of America by Hiraeth Publishing, P.O. Box 1248, Tularosa, NM, 88352. ©2024 by Hiraeth Publishing. Nothing may be reproduced in whole or in part without written permission from the authors and artists. Any similarity between places and persons mentioned in the fiction or semi-fiction and real places or persons living or dead is coincidental. Writers and artists guidelines are available online at www.hiraethsffh.com. Guidelines are also available upon request from Hiraeth Publishing, P.O. Box 1248, Tularosa, NM, 88352, if request is accompanied by a self-addressed #10 envelope with a first-class US stamp. Editor: H. David Blalock.

Contents

Stories
6	Who Put Bella Down the Wych Elm by Jasper Kent
25	Aswang by Michael Bitanga
36	O'Garretty's Companion by Sam Hicks
50	The Hungry Man by David O'Mahony
60	Something Lost by Gregory Meece
73	The Priest of Hvalsey by K. T. Booker
84	The Astrakhan Coat by Piertommaso Spagnuolo
95	The Window-Room by Jen Mierisch

Poems
24	Haunted by You by C. Payne
35	The Gift by Renee Cronley
49	Charon by Christian Dickinson
59	Will o' the Wisp by Sarah Cannavo
83	Walk On by Alan Hardy
94	Watching by DJ Tyrer

Articles
109	The Wonder of "The Thing on the Fourble Board" by Denise Noe
116	Dying Is Easy – Coming Back Is Hard by Anonymous as told to Alice Ward

Illustrations
72	Nature's Chandelier by Sonali Roy
93	Skull Crow by Warren Muzak
108	Shoe Tree by Warren Muzak

A Little Help, Please

In the world of the small indie press we fight a never-ending battle for attention to our work, as writers and in publishing. Here's an example: big publishers [you know who they are] have gobs of $$$ that they can devote to advertising and marketing. Here at Hiraeth Publishing, our advertising budget consists of the deposits for whatever soda bottles and aluminum cans we can find alongside the highways. Anti-littering laws make our task even more difficult . . . 9

That's where YOU come in. YOU are our best promoter. YOU are the one who can tell others about us. Just send 'em to our website, tell them about our store. That's all. Just that.

Of course, we don't mind if you talk us up. We're pretty good, you know. We have some award-winning and award-nominated writers and artists, plus other voices well-deserving to be heard [not everyone wins awards, right?] but our publications are read-worthy nevertheless.

That number once again is:

www.hiraethsffh.com

Friend us on Facebook at Hiraeth Publishing

Follow us on Twitter at @HiraethPublish1

What???
No subscription to
parABnormal Magazine??

We can fix that . . .
Just go here and order:
PARABNORMAL MAGAZINE SUBSCRIPTION | Hiraeth Publishing

or scan

*...also makes a great gift
any time of the year*

Who Put Bella Down the Wych Elm?
Jasper Kent

This story is inspired – no more than that – by a bit of local history from where I grew up.
The Fact

In April 1943, the skeletal remains of a woman were discovered in Hagley Wood, close to the main road between Birmingham and Kidderminster in the English Midlands. The body was crammed into the hollow trunk of an elm tree. Subsequent investigations determined that the corpse had been there for two years or more, but little further could be ascertained. The identity of the victim was never discovered, let alone that of her killer.

Eleven months later, the first graffiti appeared, chalked on a wall in nearby Birmingham.

WHO PUT BELLA DOWN THE WYCH ELM – HAGLEY WOOD

No one had given the murdered woman a name before, and there was little reason to suppose this to be anything more than an invention. But over the ensuing months, further messages appeared throughout the area, hinting at knowledge of the murder, and naming the victim 'Bella' or sometimes 'Lubella'. The spate of graffiti petered away within a year.

Four decades later, it began again. In 1984 a minor variation upon the theme was found on the wall of Hagley Village Library, followed by further occurrences across the region. The most popular site for the message, reappearing whenever it is scrubbed away, is on the base of the Georgian obelisk which stands atop Wychbury Hill, louring over the murder site itself. Always the same, familiar question:

The Fiction

There were only stars to light the hilltop, and so the towering shaft of the Monument appeared merely as an absence where it blocked them from view. The orange glow of streetlights from the villages around – Pedmore, Hagley, Wollescote – provided no real illumination.

The sudden brightness of Mrs Southill's torch flickered over the grass, zigzagging, desperate to fix on some permanent object through the darkness. There was a flash of stonework, quickly lost; another, this time with a curving white line across it: the 'B' of 'Bella'. The movements became more precise, homing in on the patchwork of bricks in disparate shades of sandstone, about halfway up the obelisk.

Slowly she tilted her wrist downwards. I could see the beam now, reflected off the minuscule droplets of water that hung in the air. When it was near horizontal, she stopped.

'Still there,' she said.

I'd never doubted it – though perhaps I'd hoped. The circle of light was broad enough to reveal only the first two words: *WHO PUT* ... She began to track the torch across the stonework, judging quite precisely the speed at which I was able to read the words. Not that I needed to read them – I knew the phrase by heart. Somehow though, in the dark of night, the letters looked different, more jagged – angrier. Maybe they'd been scrubbed off since the last time I was here, and then repainted by a different hand. It was superfluous, but I felt compelled to ask the familiar question out loud.

'*Who put Bella in the Wych Elm?*'

The graffiti vanished as Mrs Southill moved her torch again, scanning the ground around us once more.

'How close was the fire?' she asked.

'It seemed like it was all round the Monument,' I said. 'Feet away, but ...'

It couldn't have been more than half an hour earlier

that I'd been looking out of my bedroom window up at the hilltop, enfolded in darkness. It was just the same as – what? – twenty-two years before; the night of my fifth birthday. There'd been no moon then either, so all I could make out was the ring of fire around the base of the tower and the figures swaying rhythmically in its glow. Tonight, I'd again seen dancers, or had it been just the flickering of the flames?

'I'd have said so too, but there's no trace here.' She cast the torch beam in a broader search, but it revealed no ashes blackening the dewy grass. 'Did your folks see it?'

Of course they hadn't; not that time, not this time. Mine was the only bedroom at the back of the house, the only one that looked out on to Wychbury Hill, and from which the Monument could be seen. That's why, when I was a kid, I'd always thought of it as somehow *mine* – within the family, at least. I'd told them in the morning about the fire – that first time, when I was five – but they hadn't believed me. They wouldn't let me go up and look, even though it was one of our regular walks.

This time, I hadn't waited till morning. I'd set off straight up there. I was lucky to bump into Mrs Southill, just leaving her house, torch in hand.

'Alishba?' she'd asked, peering at me through the darkness. 'Where are you off to at this hour?'

'Up to the Monument.'

'You saw the fire too?'

I nodded. 'I was looking up at the hill.'

'And wondering about poor Bella, I'll be bound.'

I couldn't deny it. Mrs Southill was a self-styled guardian of local history – knew every legend there was about the body found stuffed into a Wych Elm during the war. That's why I'd gone to her when things started getting a little weird. It saved a lot of explaining now. We'd marched onwards together towards the peak of Wychbury Hill.

The first weird thing wasn't really that odd at all. What's that saying? Once is happenstance ...? It had been years before, after I'd left home and before I'd come back. I'd been on holiday in Rome with my then boyfriend Martin, on a bus heading out of the city to visit the catacombs, when something caught my eye. The place is so lousy with graffiti you scarcely pay it any notice. It must have been that one word that caught my eye: 'Bella'. For anyone from Pedmore or Hagley that name, and daubed on a wall too, well ... it added up. I turned my head and saw it, clear as day, just for an instant, spray-painted on a concrete wall.

WHO PUT BELLA IN THE WYCH ELM?

I pushed my way to the front of the bus and jumped off as soon as I could, running back to the spot.

Behind I could hear Martin calling, 'Ali!' but I wasn't going to wait for him. I got back there. Again, my eye caught on that one word, as if searching for it always. 'Bella.'

I was disappointed – relieved maybe – to read the whole thing.

SEI BELLA COME UN GOL AL 90

I tried to make sense of it, but my Italian wasn't up to much. It clearly wasn't a translation of the words on the Wychbury Monument. I looked around. I'd lost Martin somewhere along the way. A couple of guys were walking past – about my age – chatting.

'*Scusi!* You speak English?'

'*Si*,' one of them answered, grinning slyly at his friend.

'What does this mean?' I pointed.

'It says, "You are beautiful like a goal in the ninetieth!"'

'Ninetieth?'

'The ninetieth minute. Football. It's true,' he added, smiling at me. 'You are.'

I calmed down. I'd never thought myself obsessed with

the whole Wych Elm story, but if that one word could conjure up the entire sentence in my head, then maybe I was. And yet it wasn't the only piece of graffiti round here, and the wall was looking less and less like the one I'd seen from the bus. Martin was just arriving, slowing down to a walk, but I turned and continued back along the road until I found a more likely candidate – not that one stretch of stained concrete is much different from any other. There were no words here, though there must have been not long before, else why was the old lady scrubbing it clean, her dark, wrinkled face scowling as she bent down to her bucket to pick up more water on her brush? She'd nearly finished, working from right to left, against the grain of the language. I walked along. She'd only got one letter still to erase.

It looked pretty much like a 'W'.

'More like Smallbrook Street than Rome.' Mrs Southill's words brought me back from my reverie, from the sunny warmth of a *strada* in Italy to the cold darkness of a hilltop in the English autumn night. Her torch was again on the writing.

'Yes,' I said warily. Smallbrook Street had been the second thing.

I'd needed to do some research in Birmingham for my PhD, and so it had made sense to come back home, to sleep in my old bedroom where I could look out at the hill. My parents were overjoyed of course, and I was happy to be home again, happier even than as a child, knowing this time around I could leave whenever I chose.

For my doctorate I was looking into urban redevelopment in the '30s and '40s, and Birmingham seemed like a perfect case study. The reference library had thousands of photos of the streets as they'd once been – before the Blitz and before the city planners began their great redesign. I wasn't too surprised to find it chalked on a wall in one of the images – Smallbrook Street as it used to be before it was bombed. It was the usual message about Bella, like on the Monument, like I'd imagined in

Rome. They'd popped up everywhere in the '40s, as much in Birmingham as round here, closer to where the body was found.

It was later, in the middle of that night, when it struck me. I just woke up knowing, like I'd pieced it together in a dream. Smallbrook Street was flattened by a raid in 1940, so the picture must have been taken before that. But Bella's body was only discovered in 1943. It might possibly have been 1940 when she was killed, but no one would have known a thing about it – no one but the killer. Could he have written those words just to taunt the police – the world in general – about a murder that hadn't yet been discovered?

That was when I looked up Mrs Southill. I remembered her from church. My parents were – still are – Christians, which raised a few eyebrows. The expectation was that we'd be Muslim or Hindu; Sikh at a push – no one much cared which. But once the initial shock was over, everyone was very welcoming. Me and my brother got dragged along too, though it didn't take with either of us. But I remembered Mrs Southill and how she was the go-to person for local history.

I told her my theory: that the killer had been bragging about his work long before anyone knew that Bella was dead, or even that she'd once been alive.

'How long before?' was her first question.

'Three years.'

'You're sure of that?'

'It can't have been less; the street was bombed in 1940. Could have been more, I suppose.'

'Unlikely,' Mrs Southill replied, shaking her head. 'They estimated she'd been dead for eighteen months. Three years is possible, but not very much longer.'

'So this must have been done right after the murder.'

'Not necessarily.' Mrs Southill's voice was cautious, not, I felt, because she doubted her own words, but fearful of dampening my ego.

'But you said it couldn't have been much longer. And

whoever wrote it must have known about Bella's murder.'

'We can know about things in the future as well as in the past.'

I snorted, but realized I was being rude. I remembered from my childhood that beyond her interest in local folklore, she held a fascination for the paranormal. Perhaps the two things were inseparable. She guessed my objection.

'I'm not saying whoever wrote the message was psychic – though we shouldn't discount it out of hand. I meant that we can all foresee the future to the extent that we know what we intend it to be.'

It took me a moment to untwist her words, but then their meaning hit me as a knot contorting my stomach.

'You mean he wrote what he was *planning* to do?' Somehow it seemed worse; not merely to kill, not simply to brag about it, but to be so cold-hearted as to conceive it in advance, down to the very detail of where to dispose of the body, and with such certainty that he could confidently announce his crime to the world while it was no more than a notion in his head.

'A possibility. But if true, it does have implications for the more recent outbreak of graffiti.'

'Recent? You mean on the Monument?'

'Hardly. That one must be as old as you are.'

She was exactly right. It had first appeared in 1993 – the year I was born.

'There've been more?' I asked.

Mrs Southill nodded. 'We keep track of these things, and of late there has been a marked rise in sightings of "Bella". I mean the word, of course – not the individual. There must be a reason.'

'"We"?' I asked.

'Local historians such as myself. There's a website. Let me show you.'

She went to fetch her laptop, leaving me struggling to get my head around what she was suggesting. She could well have been right that the chalked text in Smallbrook

Street was a genuine portent of the murder, but was she seriously proposing that these new messages were intended to announce a fresh killing? It was preposterous on every level.

She returned and showed me the site. There were plenty of photographs, several of locations I recognized, each with the familiar question scrawled in plain view. There was no variation here. No mention of Hagley Wood; no calling her Lubella. It was all just the same as on the Monument – *Who put Bella in the Wych Elm?*

'There must be more of them that we've simply missed,' explained Mrs Southill. 'They're washed away pretty sharpish.'

I remembered the old woman in Rome and the rasping of her scrubbing brush against the concrete. I could picture her face as though it had been yesterday.

'You should get a copy of that photo of Smallbrook Street to upload,' she suggested. 'It would stir things up a bit.'

I promised her I would, and we left matters at that. In my memory, she'd always seemed a little strange, and this reacquaintance had done nothing to dispel the idea. But I couldn't hold that against her; her local knowledge was unsurpassed – and that was what I needed from her. Besides, I felt somewhere inside me the stirrings of the professional historian's disdain for the amateur, and didn't like myself for it.

It was about a week later that she phoned me. I hadn't got round to ordering a copy of the Smallbrook Street photo and as soon as I heard her voice I started trying to come up with some excuse for why not. But it wasn't that she was calling about.

'I've found something,' she said.

'About Bella? Tell me!'

'More interesting if I show you. Meet me at the church in half an hour.'

It was a steep climb up to St Peter's, built on the lower slopes of Wychbury Hill. Mrs Southill's house wasn't far off, and she was already waiting for me at the lychgate, its wooden-beamed arch supported on ancient stone walls. The word reminded me of 'Wych' – Wych Elm, Wychbury Hill. A lych was a corpse, rested here at the gate on the way to its funeral. I wasn't sure what 'wych' meant, though everyone insisted it had nothing to do with black magic.

She led me through and up the path towards the church. This was where we'd first met, at some Sunday service, a quarter of a century before. The memory was suddenly vivid.

'You must be young Alishba, mustn't you?' she'd said, smiling down at me. 'We've all heard so much about you.' I remembered being puzzled at what she meant, who she could have heard anything from, but I'd come to realize it was just one of those things grown-ups say. She'd gone on to tell me what a pretty name it was and begun a long explanation of its biblical origins.

'Penny for them?'

I realized I'd been smiling at the recollection. 'I was miles away,' I replied. 'Or rather years. You asked if I'd been named after Aaron's wife.'

'Did I? Her name was ... let me see ... Elisheba! Yes, I suppose it must be the same. I'd quite forgotten.'

We were at the church now, at the eastern end, away from the main entrance. Mrs Southill marched off to the left, circling around the building. I remembered how we'd always gone that way to get to the porch, yet carried on in the same direction when leaving after the service. It was bad luck to walk withershins – anticlockwise – around a church.

Evidently – and unsurprisingly – Mrs Southill shared the superstition; our journey took us the long way round, almost back to where we'd started.

'Here!' she announced, pointing at a nondescript patch of the local red sandstone, so familiar in buildings round here. The church was originally Norman, but had been reconstructed many times over. The scratches crisscrossing the stonework had been there long enough to be weathered almost smooth again.

'It doesn't show directly, of course,' she continued, 'but I've got a trick for that.' She reached into her little rucksack and brought out a dark blue crayon, the sort children use to draw, but with all the paper torn off. For a moment I thought she was going to start scribbling on the wall herself, creating new Bella graffiti to upload to her website. But she delved in again and brought out a sheet of paper, placing it against the wall.

'Hold this,' she said, 'just where I have it.'

I did as I was told and she gently rubbed the side of the crayon against the paper, and through it the sandstone. The surface began to turn blue, but not evenly. Where the texture of the church wall was pitted, the crayon didn't catch, revealing the pattern that had been so hard to read in the stone itself. And it *was* a pattern – no random jumble of scratches, but clear, straight lines and smooth curves. It couldn't be described as tidy, but it most certainly revealed intent.

As soon as I realized they were letters, I knew what they would say. It was 'IN THE' that appeared first – Mrs Southill was working outwards from the centre. Once 'BELLA' appeared on the left, the paper was full. She took out another sheet and I held it for her just as I had the first. It took three to encompass the full text, in lettering about two inches high. There were other marks too, arbitrary lines cutting across the words as the stone revealed the strata of its history, but they were unable to obscure the message.

'How did you know?' was all I could ask. It was obvious that she had gone through this process already and was aware what her actions would reveal, but she could not have assessed every brick of the edifice this way, patiently hoping to find something meaningful.

'You look like you could use a drink,' she said.

I couldn't argue with her. I felt drained by the shock. What I thought I'd seen in Rome I could put down to an over-active imagination. The photograph of Smallbrook Street was a clue in an historical puzzle. But seeing the letters here, so ancient as to be almost worn away, caused me to shudder. It was eerie – uncanny.

We walked back to her house. She made us both coffee and then poured me a shot of something that smelled of alcohol and unfamiliar spices. I sipped it, but I was already beginning to calm. Those scratched words were not necessarily as ancient as they appeared. How should I know the rate sandstone erodes? And it might not even have been a natural process. A few minutes with a jet-washer could easily give a fresh inscription the patina of centuries.

'Drink up,' she said. 'It will do you good.'

I downed the liquor and felt a wave of heat as the alcohol cascaded over the walls of my stomach. It wasn't unpleasant, but I kept hold of the glass so that she wouldn't feel obliged to refill it.

'You asked how I knew,' she said.

I nodded. 'Did you remember it, from when it was clearer?'

She looked at me over her spectacles. 'I'm hardly that old.' She went across to the bookshelf and picked off a battered hardback. 'I've had this for years, but I'd never really looked at it closely.' She handed it to me.

Medieval Churches of Staffordshire, Warwickshire and Worcestershire.

It was a large format, requiring both my hands to hold it. From the dust jacket I guessed it was published in the '60s. There were black and white photos of various churches, but I didn't recognize any of them.

'I've marked the place,' she said.

A yellow Post-it Note protruded from between the leaves. I slid my finger in and opened the book. The page was filled with a print of a church. A caption explained what it was.

St Peter's, Pedmore. Woodcut. Early C16.

We'd been there just minutes before. I looked again. I

wouldn't have recognized it without the prompt – it was a rudimentary depiction, and rebuilding work had made the current structure something rather different. But the tower was clear enough, and that allowed me to work out how everything else fitted.

'You'll need this.'

I glanced up. Mrs Southill was holding out her hand, offering me a magnifying glass.

'Where should I look?'

I could almost hear her tut. 'Where do you suppose?'

It was obvious what she meant. The view was of the north side of the church, the same side we'd been on. I recalled the spot we had stood at, just beside one of the buttresses. They were clear to see. And there was something there, as fine a detail as a woodcut could convey, too small for me to make out. I used the eyeglass. The image moved rapidly from side to side until my hand steadied.

The engraver hadn't bothered with a precise reproduction, but it was enough – enough to convey the existence of the text he must have read when familiarizing himself with his subject. Only the initial letters were shown in any detail, the important ones: a 'W', a 'P', a 'B', another 'W' and an 'E'.

'Puts us back rather earlier than 1940, don't you agree?'

'What can it mean?'

She shrugged. 'There are natural explanations of course ... but they rely on coincidence.'

'Such as?'

'Well, suppose that this wording is just some local piece of argot – a phrase used by children for centuries at a level too low to become common knowledge, but sufficient to be passed on. Every so often, perhaps every few decades or once in a century, it surfaces and we see an outbreak of these scrawlings – scratched, chalked or spray-painted as the era dictates.'

'But what about the murder? What about Bella

herself?'

'Who's to say the victim was called Bella? She could have been anybody. They found a body in a Wych Elm, for sure. But that could have been just another coincidence.'

I raised an eyebrow.

'Or perhaps someone was inspired by the phrase. Not inspired to kill, but having killed they saw it as an apt place to put the body.'

I thought about it. It was possible, but ...

'It's hard to believe that there's so little connection,' I said. 'Between the graffiti and the body.'

'I think you'll prefer it to my other explanation.'

'And what's that?'

'That there is every connection between them. That all the messages concerning Bella, from the Middle Ages, to the war, to the one upon the Monument today – and countless others lost or forgotten – refer to that same occasion; to the dreadful sacrifice which took place in Hagley Wood.'

It sounded like bullshit, but still I listened.

'Today, even science accepts that time and space are one and the same. But what, I wonder, are their relative scales? If a murder in Hagley can provoke the chalking of a message ten miles away on a street in Birmingham, then why not on a church wall many centuries away in time, but in distance much closer, in Pedmore. Who can say which is truly further for the vibrations of such an horrific event to emanate?'

'So Bella's death was remembered ... before it happened?'

'Oh, I don't pretend to understand, but just because Bella's body was discovered in the Wych Elm in 1943, it doesn't mean her death was a single event that occurred a few months before. That is merely the moment at which it impinged upon mortal consciousness. It's as though ...' She paused for a moment, choosing her words. '... as though a pipe has sprung a leak. The rupture appears at a single point, and yet water is drained from the entire length of the pipe. Witches and demons gather eagerly around the breach. A hundred yards distant – or a hundred years – is better than to be utterly disconnected. And if that disruption can be nourished, then it will grow stronger, and both time and distance will matter less, and those who form their congregation around it will feel closer still.'

She stopped, then looked at me with a smile of self-deprecation. 'You know, when I say it out loud, it becomes less convincing. Perhaps a few coincidences should be allowed if they facilitate a more acceptable explanation.' She was breathing heavily, exhausted by the passion of her speech.

'I should go,' I said.

'Yes. Yes. That would be for the best. But think about what we've discussed. Not that fancy about space and time, but about what we saw at the church, and how else it might be explained.'

That had been two days ago, and I'd thought about it a lot, without any conclusion. The beam of Mrs Southill's torch ascended gradually to the summit of the Monument, leaving the remainder of the hilltop invisible, stretching away from us in all directions. Yet still I could see the letters on the base, somehow now luminescent. Was it possible, what she had said, that they had not been put there *after* Bella's death, but in some sense *around* it? That words written decades later were equivalent to those inscribed earlier – centuries earlier?

'There's nothing here,' I said. 'We should go down.'

'Not yet.' There was an edge in her voice.

'I must have been mistaken ... about the fire.'

'I saw it too.'

'I suppose so.' And then it occurred to me. Her house was closer to the Monument than mine, near the church, upon Wychbury Hill itself, which meant she had no view of it. There was no way she could have seen what I saw, not if she'd been home.

'Look! There!' she hissed.

I followed her gaze. A fire had sprung up, somewhere near the woods, maybe fifty yards away.

'And there!'

We both turned to witness another blaze flaring in almost the opposite direction. I could see figures between us and the flames.

'What's happening?' I gasped.

'A sabbat,' she said, her voice filled with awe.

'What? You mean ... witches?' I tried to laugh, but it was unconvincing.

'I told you, they like to gather. It's only just down the other side of the hill.'

'Why here, then? Why not go there?'

'My dear Alishba, they're here because of you.'

'Of me?'

'You, Elisheba, wife of Aaron. It's strange how a word can change over the years, isn't it – over the millennia?'

Another fire erupted, to the right, and then a fourth. We were surrounded now.

'These Hebrew names never quite make it into the modern world untouched.'

I didn't look at Mrs Southill as she spoke. My eyes were on those dark silhouettes amongst the flames. They were approaching.

'Elisheba gives us Isabelle,' she continued, as if talking to a class of schoolchildren. 'Or Isabella.'

I turned to look at her. Her features were lengthened and distorted by the light from the torch, raised high above her head. 'Or Bella.'

As she spoke that final word, she brought the torch crashing down on to my skull.

***

It must be a good few hours I've lain here unconscious; the moon has had time to rise. I'm just where I was, lying in the grass not far from the Monument. I can see it clearly now, thrusting into the sky. I reach up and cautiously touch my temple, but there's no hint of a bruise.

I haul myself to my feet. The fires have gone and in the moonlight I can clearly see the little clusters of woodland where they had been. I am where I was, yet everything is somehow different. I look around, trying to get my bearings, but the glow of streetlights from the surrounding villages has faded. Other things have altered too. There used to be a fence around the Monument, keeping visitors at a safe distance. Now, anyone could walk up and touch it.

And then I notice the greatest metamorphosis: the spray-painted words on its base have vanished.

It's time to go, but without the usual clues, I have no idea which way is home. Although from here there is only one direction of travel: downhill. I set off.

Before I get very far, I hear a sound – a low buzzing overhead, the drone of an aeroplane. Not the familiar hum of a jet, but the whirring of old-fashioned propellers.

I continue downwards and at last reach a landmark – a road. Still there are no streetlights, but I'm pretty sure it's the Birmingham Road. I've chosen the wrong side of the hill, but at least I know the route home. I hear another low rumble – a car this time. I look up and down the road, but at first I can't see it. When I do, it's not what I expect.

For one thing, it's some old vintage model, with a big grill and bulbous wheel arches. A pair of round headlamps stick out from either side of the bonnet, but there's something not right about them. As the car passes I can see more clearly. Each light is covered by its own little canopy, directing its beam down upon the road ahead and nowhere else. I remember this sort of thing from school. It was how they did things for the blackout – how they did things during the war.

The car stops, then backs up until it's level with me.

'Need a lift?' The man's face is illuminated by the dashboard. He's about my age. His hat only confirms the era in which I've found myself. In a world entirely strange to me, what threat can one stranger be? I climb in with a mumbled thanks. We set off.

'And what might your name be?' he asks.

'Bella.' I'm not sure why that word comes from my mouth. Perhaps I'm worried that he'll find Alishba a little too ... foreign.

He chuckles to himself. 'Astonishing.'

'What is?'

He says nothing, but a moment later the car is turning right on to a narrow lane. There's a wood on one side and a field on the other.

'What are you doing?' I ask.

'Got to turn round if I'm going to take you home to Pedmore.'

But we don't turn around. We carry on down the little road. I'm no more surprised at it than I am at his knowing I come from Pedmore. His face seems familiar, as does his voice, but it's not that. I understand now where we are. That's Hagley Wood on our right. It's obvious where we're going.

We pull up and he steps out, opening the door for me like a gentleman, though I suspect it's to make sure I don't run. But what would be the point – where would I run to?

He leads me into the wood – only a few hundred yards. I see flames flickering in the distance and for once they do not vanish as we approach.

And finally, there it is – the Wych Elm. It's a strange thing. Ancient – cut back a hundred times and allowed to regrow. Thick, strong limbs extend upwards, with a mass of more puny branches, little more than sticks, intertwining around its base, forming a nest. There looks to be plenty of room inside.

I recognize some of the horde that have gathered, small groups each around its own bonfire, the fires themselves circling the tree: people I've met during my life, some incidentally, some I've known more closely. I'm happier to note those who are not here, yet might have been: my parents for example, people I've regarded as friends – though some of those are present.

The man who delivered me to this place I now realize

is my ex-boyfriend Martin, or someone very like him. He didn't seem to recognize me when he picked me up, even though he was expecting me to be there – had made sure to drive past at precisely the appointed time.

There's an old woman here too whose face is entirely familiar – the same woman I'd seen scrubbing that wall in Rome, perhaps only minutes after writing the message up herself. Is she still Italian, in this place, in this era? Or doesn't it work like that?

'You must be young Alishba, mustn't you?' The most familiar face of all – the one I've seen most recently – smiles at me benignly. 'We've all heard so much about you.'

'Hello again, Mrs Southill,' I reply, but this is not her younger self. It is *her*self, the same soul, but in a different aeon.

'Southill?' The smile broadens. 'Always such a boon, to learn something of what we will become, or have been.'

A few of the other faces look at me expectantly, as if I might provide them with some similar tidbit of information, but most of them are strangers. Those I recognize, I choose not to enlighten.

'But that is not our prime concern.' Mrs Southill looks at me, her face abruptly sombre. 'Now Bella, wife of the high priest, sister-in-law to the Lawgiver, this is not the first time you have come this way, nor will it be the last. But each time I must ask the same question.'

I suddenly find it all so familiar. She is right; I have been here before, time and again, though always a different me – just as this is a different Mrs Southill. It is my ... our destiny. I take no comfort in knowing that I shall pass this way countless times more – if past and future have any meaning at this juncture. The ritual is familiar, and I know my part. I have rehearsed a thousand times.

'Ask it,' I say.

There is a hush, allowing Mrs Southill to speak. 'Who,' she asks, 'will put Elisheba in her resting place?'

I step forward towards the Wych Elm, pushing the branches aside, which yield willingly to me. My feet scrabble against stubble around its base and my shoe comes off, but it doesn't matter. Soon I am inside, surrounded by nature; swaddled by her. Through the dense leaves I still see the flames, see them flickering in the ecstatic eyes of my worshippers.

I pull my knees up to my chest, and let my head fall forward, and sleep.

Haunted by You
C. Payne

Here I stay, ethereal
Always and forever bound
Unseen, but not un-felt
Never more than a step away, I
Touch you gently as you sleep
Envious of the warmth
Death has stolen from me

Between worlds, I
Yearn for you

You think me gone,
Our love interred
Unaware that I'm haunted by you

Aswang
Michael Bitanga

People love to point their unknowing fingers at the house. Say it's cursed. Haunted. Thinking the blame can be boxed up neatly in wood and brick. But it wasn't the house that was haunted.

Sandra, Adrian, and their daughter Scarlett Alonto moved from small town Tofte, Minnesota to the picturesque suburbs of San Diego, California. With Adrian's well-earned promotion, they were able to get a brand new house with all the fixings. Close to 2,000 square feet of freedom. They adjusted quite nicely. As if they've always been here.

They zipped through all the tourist attractions–Balboa Park, San Diego Zoo, SeaWorld, Petco Park–earning their San Diego badges. And down the list they went.

One of their favorites was the elegantly somber Whaley House. The daytime tour wasn't anything special. Their tour guide, Anthony, was a middle-aged man with only a few sparks left from when he used to be passionate about his job.

But being in a relic with so much history made the family feel like time travelers. Pioneers traversing the past. And Scarlett wasn't scared once, even with the tour guide's usually effective ghost stories. They didn't see a translucent orb or feel their hair erect in the presence of *something* despite all the promises. Which is typically the case for places like this.

"The only haunted house you'll get a bang for your buck is in Disneyland," Adrian told his family.

Scarlett had a bursting light in her. It was bright with every single thing she did. Soccer, dancing, singing, dunking Oreos, drawing mini horses with big bows–her artistic specialty. Even throwing a fit. Every. Single. Thing. Until she turned eight.

Now, that light is dimming. Of course, all of our lights fade as we rack up the mileage. But we hold onto it for as long as we can. And we find other things to keep it shining. To make it brighter. Like comfortable friendships, theme park adventures, our favorite flicks, songs that hold special moments in time within their notes, and, of course, our furry four-legged family members. But a light that starts to dim at eight? That's too soon. For anybody.

Several nights a week, Scarlett complains about a monster that lives in the darkness under her bed. *Typical complaint of an eight-year-old*, the Alontos thought. *She'll get over it.*

Usually, it just stares. A vacant gaze and a smile that's more grimace than human. If she squints perfectly enough, she can make out the two dull lanterns in the sea of black. And a hand waving her into the abyss.

Sometimes Sandra thought it was the Whaley House visit that clawed roots into her mind. But that was over two years ago. She feared it may be something worse. Something she inherited.

***

For months, Mom would come to the rescue. She flips on the lights and it vanishes like a magic trick. Nothing under Scarlett's bed but dust bunnies and cookie crumbs. But this night was different.

Scarlett punctuated the very corner of her bed farthest from the edge. She closes her eyes, but can't unsee the figure bathing in the dark of her mind. And the smell. The smell is new to her. Cheap perfume trying desperately to mask fresh roadkill.

She imagines the creature's arms elongating. Extending like greasy snakes slithering toward her. Wrapping her up and squeezing her until she's rigid and purple. The rancid scent gets stronger, intoxicating her frail body. Her legs enter the creature's mouth. Then her torso. Then her head. Until she's gone. Scarlett's not just devoured. She imagines she becomes the creature. Drowns in its malicious thoughts filled with hopeless voices and screams that ride the fence of delight and terror.

Then she opens her eyes. She can hear its playful taps on the hardwood floor underneath her.

"Moooooom!!!" Scarlett yells out like a battle cry. Tearful, but feral. She curls into a ball, hiding behind a raggedy teddy bear with a single button eye.

Scarlett shuts her eyes but still sees the shape waiting within the cavernous abyss under her bed. It's breathing heavy. Salivating. Smiling at her with cloudy spheres. Waiting for Scarlett to rescue another toy. Its smile is primordial. A showing of teeth.

It whispers.

"Come here, cuddle bunny. It's okay." Its fingernails drum the floor. "I'm here now." It sounds...familiar. Heavy footsteps creak closer. Sandra appears at Scarlett's doorway. She's just a shape standing there. Still as a mannequin.

"What is it, hun? You okay?"

She usually flips the light on before a single word slips out of her mouth. But all she does is stand there. Her silhouette breathing heavily. Yet she doesn't move at all. Just stillness. Her breathing eats up the silence.

Scarlett's too afraid to move. A million pins stab her toes.

The figure of her mom inches closer. Closer. "I'm here now." *It sounds like Mommy....* But her voice is too calm. And unnaturally kind. Like a celebrity doing a late night talk show interview.

She sits on the bed. Perfect posture. Tapping the space beside her. "It's okay. I'm here now."

She sits criss-cross applesauce on the bed, caressing the spot next to her with a precise gentleness. Scarlett can barely make out the details of her face in the dark. Every move she makes is mimicry.

"Moooooom!!!" Scarlett vomits out. Eyes closed. Face scrunched

Whoever was on her bed is gone. But a subtle

depression on the bedding remains. Sandra appears at her doorway with tired eyes and a yawn. *Mom?*

"There's...something under my bed. Then it was on my bed. I don't know where it went. It was..it was talking to me."

"What did it say?" Sandra takes a step forward into enough moonlight to show her face.

"It called me...'cuddle bunny.'"

Sandra's sleepy eyes widen.

"It's okay. I'm here now," Sandra said with a warm smile, extending her arm. Scarlett stays put.

"It's..it's under there again. I-I think."

Sandra stands stiff next to the bed. She lowers to her creaky knees.

"Be careful, Mom," Scarlett whispered.

A terrible pulse in Sandra's stomach thumps hard, as if some unborn monster is trying to tear its way into reality.

"It's okay," Sandra said, taking one more look at Scarlett's beady eyes filled with dread.

Her stomach is volcanic. The fear flows through her guts, torching the lining. She lowers her head. Its milky orbs fill Sandra's eyes, turning them into a galaxy of darkness.

Sandra stays right in front of it. Dead center. It looks...like *her*. Like all the bad parts of her magnified and mutated.

She takes a long, soothing deep breath in. Then she deflates. *Confidence is just love facing fear.*

"There's nothing here, baby. Come look," Sandra said. The creature smiles, drool spilling onto the floor, tilting its head with eagerness.

"Are you sure?"

"Of course. Come look."

Scarlett crawls to the edge of the bed. She lowers both feet to the frigid floor. The creature inhales her scent to the point of euphoria. Scarlett sees her mom's head half-buried under the bed.

"C'mon, hun. There's nothing here," Sandra reassured her. She holds the creature's gaze, peering deeper into its cloudy eyes.

"Remember me?" the creature whispered to Sandra. Its eerie smile is nostalgic.

Sandra thought this was something different. Something that belonged to Scarlett alone.

She almost forgot about it. Wished she could. But the memories of the creature flood her mind, suffocating her with the part of her childhood she thought she buried so deep it would take a bad miracle to resurface. It vanished when her father left. And now it found its way back with Scarlett.

"Can I turn on the light?" asked Scarlett, tip-toeing with her voice.

"Remember what I told you?"

"If you can face it in the dark, you are the light."

"That's right, baby. C'mon and look."

Scarlett lowers her head to peek under her bed, gripping her teddy bear. She looks around, scanning every sector of the dark space.

Sandra locks onto the creature's gaze. Its breath gets heavier, dragging air into its teeth.

"You're right! It's gone!" Scarlett yelled.

Sandra smiles back at the creature. It retreats into the abyss. Its heavy breathing gets smaller. Smaller. Until the silence consumes it.

"See, I told ya!" Sandra picks up Scarlett and plops her back onto her bed, tucking her back into safety.

"It's gone now. I made sure. You made sure. All good. Okay?"

"But what if it comes back?"

"Yell and I'll come running." She winks at Scarlett.

"But what if you're not here?"

"FaceTime me and slide your phone under the bed."

"Or...I mean, when you're *gone* gone."

Sandra sits on the bed and looks deeply into Scarlett's eyes, gently caressing her cheek, seeing forever.

"Then you'll be able to take care of it. For you and your own kiddos. But I'm not going anywhere for a long time, okay?"

"Promise?"

Sandra's eyes drop down. Then she picks them back up, catching Scarlett's curious gaze.

"I'll always be here for you. Even when I'm not."

"How?"

"Love."

Sandra gives Scarlett the biggest hug. As if she'll never see her again. How she always hugs her.

"And I love you so so so so much." She leans in, pressing a warm, comforting kiss to her forehead.

Sandra slips back into her own bed. She hugs her side pillow, feeling the cool cloud against her skin. Thoughts of her daughter dance in her mind. A smile stretches across her face as her eyes droop down, closing up shop.

The hardwood floor beneath her bed moans as she's drifting away, pulling her back into the night. A slow breath breaks the heavy silence. That frozen, over-stretched smile is creeping back into her mind.

As long as it's here and not there, she thought. *I'll keep it under my bed as long as I can. So long that it dies there. And if I can't keep it there long enough...I'll teach my cuddle bunny how to kill it..as many times as she has to.*

She slides out of her bed and sits criss-cross applesauce, waiting for the creature with a bulletproof smile.

It peeks its head out just enough so Sandra can see it. It looks like Scarlett. But older. Maybe in her 20s. It crawls toward her. Its skin is dry, bruised. Track marks wrapped around her scrawny arms. Its sunken eyes catch Sandra's. Her smile disintegrates.

"Help me. Mommy, help me," it says with a thirsty, stale voice. Like she hasn't spoken to anyone for months. "Why didn't you help me?" It touches the blistering needle hole on its arm.

"You didn't. You could have. But you let them get me.

Didn't you? So you could be safe. So you could continue your life. Follow dreams you let go. You knew if they had me they wouldn't bother with you. You left me. YOU LEFT ME! Just like your dad."

"No," Sandra whispers. Tears escape, streaming down the creases of her face. Tracing the history of her pain. Sandra shuts her eyes.

She slips back to thoughts of Scarlett going to middle school. Laughing with friends. Graduating college. Getting her first job. Scarlett's smile is invincible. It fills her up with light.

"Moooooom!!!!" Scarlett's yell floods down the hall. Sandra opens her eyes and bursts to her bedroom door. Her hands strangle the knob, trying to open it. She rams it with her shoulder, bruising it with every bang.

"Mommy!!!" Scarlett's voice explodes and crackles.

Sandra breaks her door open and races to Scarlett's room. She should be a little ball wrapped in her blanket nesting at the corner of her bed against the wall. But the room is only filled with the remnants of her scream.

Sandra kneels down and peers into the darkness beneath the bed. It isn't just shadows down there anymore —it's a thick, oily abyss. A chill slips out of it, pulling her closer, challenging her to enter the unknown. To find her helpless daughter before the darkness fully consumes her.

Confidence is just love facing fear, she thought. Heart pounding. Fists clenched so hard her knuckles are bone white.

She slips into the abyss under the bed. Into a frigid, endless nothingness that consumes. A thousand different voices swarm her, as she walks through, trying to hear Scarlett's voice cut through it all. Sandra keeps walking. Cautious. When she looks back, Scarlett's bedroom is gone. There is only nothingness all around.

In the morning, the sun beams through the windows of the Alonto house. Birds chirp their greatest hits. But the nest is empty. Adrian comes home drained from work. After finding Sandra's keys, smartphone, and wallet on her bedside table, he storms into every room of the house, calling for Sandra and Scarlett. Only the birds answer. He checks the front door security camera. Then the garage security camera. No trace of them. Adrian gets the police on the phone while banging on his neighbor's door. He vomits out his concerns to the cops. They aloofly tell him a police cruiser is coming by.

By the time they arrived, Adrian had spoken to all his neighbors, their friends, the parents of Scarlett's friends, and her school principal. Nobody knows a thing. So he unloads on the police with a rage fueled by a seemingly endless fear.

***

A few months later, Adrian sold the house and used the money to fund any and every effort to find them. He couldn't rest there with all the good memories along with the unknown terrors that took his family. And he went to the local news with his eerie story. Since then, their house has become a local attraction. Various rumors arise about the house. Many say it's cursed. Haunted. A portal to hell. Like that.

Donald Fluttner, the portly business shark who bought the house, said he would give 20% of merchandise sales to fund Adrian's search efforts. Adrian never signed a contract and never saw a dime.

The place is filled with eager tour guides and curious guests. Cheap souvenirs and promotion for the new film drown out the family memories. *The Scarlett House* is number one on every San Diego's Best Attractions list, beating even the Whaley House.

Adrian knew in the deep, dark, hollow part of his soul, where the truth often hides, that he would never get to hold his family in his arms again. A six-pack sweating on the motel table and a fistful of cheap pills helped him see Sandra and Scarlett. Hold them in his mind. The dark hours stretch on, as Adrian rots away until the gray light of dawn arrives, unforgiving and empty. The cycle continued until hope became so small and brittle you can step on it without noticing.

***

Three years passed. Like the snap of fingers.

Adrian, crumbling in his own worship of the bottle, is passed out with shades on in his grimy motel room. He's been there so long he could hear the furniture talk in between the nightly visitors bleeding his wallet. A phone call from the front desk rattles him awake. Scarlett was found at the San Onofre State Beach by the local authorities.

For Scarlett, three years felt like a long, drawn-out night. She remembers creatures that morphed endlessly, babbling to her and Sandra through a kaleidoscope of voices. Some familiar. Some lonely. Some wild and vicious. Trying to plant in their minds that there was only one way out of the void–a lone door that can only be opened with the twist of a knife. Being there was like trying to make out the horizon of the ocean at night–except day never came to make things clear. To prove that time exists. So she focused on her mom's soothing voice. Her beautiful face with a smile that cut through the night. That became her sun. And her warm hand intertwined with hers, clasping so tightly only God could rip them apart. Then she woke up on the beach by herself.

No drugs were in her system. Not a scratch on her body. There's still a twinkle of light in her eyes. Faint as a dying star. But still there.

Scarlett was put into foster care. She spoke sparingly, only saying what she needed to say without any fluff or excitement. She writes and draws in her journal. Spilling her thoughts into it daily.

Every weekend, Scarlett visited her dad at a halfway house. Since Scarlett's miracle return, a renewed drive to get clean and get out has taken the wheel.

Every night, just as Scarlett flips off the light and the room fills with shadows, she whispers to the darkness under her bed, hoping her mom might hear her. Maybe tonight she'll feel the gentle creak on the bed, see a familiar face rise from the gloom, and feel her mom's cozy, cosmic hug that smells like strawberries and morning coffee. She waits. Her words slipping into the silence like a prayer, hoping for a familiar voice to answer her.

She hasn't seen her mom ever since their time in the void. And she hasn't seen any monsters since then either. Besides the ones of her own kind. The ones that infest the world with their greed. And pollute the minds and morale of the weak. They're in the smiles of the slick-suited, the hollow eyes of the desperate, feeding their pitless stomachs.

Maybe those are the ones that didn't have moms, dads, aunts, and uncles. A Sandra to light the way. Easy prey, ripe for the taking. They snake into them, burrowing deep into their guts like a sickness that never leaves. Growing them up to beat on the weak with proud smiles on their faces. Steal from the poor without a hint of hesitation. Lie so smoothly they could look at you dead center and convince you the sky is red.

Scarlett never heard her Mom's voice again. But she could feel it in her bones–her Mom is out there somewhere deep in the abyss. With others who made the same sacrifice out of love unbound by time. All of them together, guarding the vast door to our world. Forging a defiant light too bright for the darkness to swallow.

The Gift
Renee Cronley

The moon is full—round and rusty,
like the pocket watch my grandfather left me.
The rhythmic ticking, like a steady heartbeat,
pulsed with a sense of impending change—
a feeling as unnerving as the whispers I've been hearing
that foretold of events I had no right to know.
My black suit is draped over the hamper, undecided—
half tucked away, exhausted from the funeral, and half
ready to rise again for an unexpected occasion.
The ticking stops and there is an ominous silence
as midnight moves into the room and the hour
opens up to a new day that feels different from the others.
A soft tap on my window shatters the quiet,
and I see my grandfather inviting me outside to meet
the faces behind the voices I've been hearing.

O'Garretty's Companion
Sam Hicks

Our introductions were done with. Now we sat in what he called "the big room," me with notepad on my knees, and he, relaxed, loose-limbed, and hands at ease upon his chair's cambered arms. My own chair had pulled me into its depths in a way that was oddly intimate; less embrace than soft restraint.

But how, I wondered, could this man have been a contemporary of Barr's? That would make him about eighty, but I'd have guessed half. A few greys showed in his dark hair and a crease or two about his eyes, but his forehead and jaw were firm and smooth, and his neck, when he turned his head, crumpled less than mine. The first thought that came to me was of Michelangelo's David, powerful and sublime, but I was surprised to later realise how brutish, how over-fleshed, that stone face really was, and how far from the image I'd always carried in my head. Perhaps O'Garretty had had surgery—such a handsome man was bound to be quite vain.

He brought his fingers into a steeple and gazed at me above them, eyes gleaming a bright and undimmed blue. "Gerda told me you have questions about Franklin Barr? For a book you're writing?"

"That's right," I tried to sit forward in the clinging chair, but it was having none of it. "There's not much useful information about him out there. It's hearsay mostly, and Gerda happened to mention you might be the only person alive who knew him well. You see, I'm writing about the British occult movements of the fifties and sixties, with an emphasis on those that developed beyond the major cities, the outliers, if you like. It's a—" My words fell away; a sudden breeze had disturbed the deep foliage outside the far window, releasing a quivering glint of such intensity that it left me momentarily blind. Blinking away the glare, I looked back to the room. It was an overcast afternoon and the gloom that had met me in the entrance hall hung just as heavily in there. Thick curtains draped the wide window, Middle Eastern rugs covered the floor, and every *objet* supporting table, and the two long sofas, were overlain by kelim throws or some variety of silky tasselled stuff. Only the splendid mahogany writing desk and chair lacked additional layers. The dim light and the rich fabrics made me think how easily sleep might come in such a room, where the muffled weight of dreams already seemed to hang in the air. O'Garretty coughed discreetly.

"Oh, yes, anyway, Franklin Barr," I said, keeping my eyes away from the window. "His name keeps cropping up in my researches, is the thing, but his influence appears to have lasted longer than any personal memories. I mean, my contacts often credit him with certain insights, certain ceremonial innovations, and yet very few seem to have met or worked with him, or if they did, so briefly that, especially given their age, what they have to say is annoyingly vague. He never published, of course, which doesn't help."

"Well, Barr wasn't what you'd call a public man." His left hand rose, languidly, to loosen his silk cravat. "His writings were only circulated privately, and rarely. But you're quite right. There's no one left who knew him well. Only myself. And my companion." And he uttered the word "companion" with a barely perceptible emphasis that made me wonder if—because he came, after all, from another age—he meant a male partner. But I dismissed the notion; Franklin Barr was known to be gay and had made no secret of it, and it was unlikely his associates would feel the need to obfuscate.

"Gerda didn't mention your companion," I said. "I was under the impression you lived alone. So they know Barr well?"

"Gerda and I have never actually met, you know," he said—and I didn't miss the side-stepping of my question. "We're not close in that way. Now and then I pass her some ephemera of Barr's for her archives, but we've only ever communicated by letter, and nowadays e-mail, which, strangely, I rather prefer. No one compares to her, do they, when it comes to sourcing rare texts? Although there's one in particular—a Persian grimoire—that she has as yet failed to find."

"Oh really? The infallible Gerda? Which grimoire is that?"

"I'm afraid that's a matter for me and her. But what you would like to ask me about Mr Barr?" He leaned his head to one side, and I felt a small, unpleasant shock. For one second, the silvery glint that I'd seen play about the garden foliage seemed, somehow, to have cast its chasing light across his face. And perhaps it was this illusion of the unearthly that made me sense, briefly, a great separation between us, and that O'Garretty's world was one a mere mortal, such as I, might never hope to visit. I'd interviewed many practitioners of the occult arts, and found them disappointingly down to earth; people who, in another life, would have made quite effective psychologists. The odd character, usually those who'd gained "a name", might affect a certain air of drama, but I'd never, until then, felt I was in the presence of someone indefinably marked by their imagined congress with the Other. It is only the truly desolate, I've found, who possess an aura, a shield, you can almost feel. But when I looked at O'Garretty I thought I might be able to reach out and touch a barrier that was clear and crystalline and as dense as permafrost.

"If we could start with the basics, if you know them," I said, opening my notebook. "Where he was born, where he grew up, how he developed the particular practice of evocation I've heard so much about. I'd like to know how he became the person he was. All I've got to go on is that his circle operated in Kent, he died from cancer in 1963, and that, reputedly, he claimed to conjure daemonic beings in corporeal form in order to converse with them. But as I say, basics first."

O'Garretty sat back in his chair. His clear gaze turned away from me and settled on a shelf of figurines—Roman and Egyptian funerary goods, I guessed—a winged and horned, half-human bestiary worked in bronze and alabaster.

"Conjure," he said, still avoiding my eye, "is not the word. Barr hated its whiff of vaudeville. But evocation was indeed his greatest power. And his claims weren't empty. But I can tell you what I know of *the basics*, as you say."

Gerda had warned me of O'Garretty's hatred for recording devices, meaning I'd spent a good part of the preceding week reviving my long-neglected shorthand, and I was half-confident that, if he wasn't a rapid speaker, I'd just about get by. But, putting pen to paper, I began to doubt my skills. Would I really be able to re-translate? Was I doing it all wrong? Luckily, as O'Garretty spoke slowly enough, indeed trailing off at several points, I could resort to longhand—although that, too, soon proved to hold its own frustrations.

Barr was born in Canterbury in 1922, I wrote, the second son of a wealthy family who'd made their money in manufacturing. He missed active service in the Second World War due to a disability that gave him no real grip in his left hand, and it was during his backroom work for the Ministry of Defence that he came into contact with members of the Ordo Templi Orientis, and, having had an interest in the mystical from a very young age, became an initiate. At this point, when O'Garretty paused, I wrote: "Pure gold!"

He knew them all O'Garretty said—Crowley, Gardner, Kenneth Grant. In fact, Barr was closely involved with Grant for a while, following both their expulsions from the O.T.O.—Grant's expulsion being a matter of record, Barr's an enduring enigma. Barr was inspired by Grant's concept of communion with forces outside the codified hierarchies, and it was at about that time, in the mid 1950s, that he developed his own path; the Gnostic system of encounter to which, O'Garretty said, I must have been referring when I spoke of his lasting influence.

My pen dropped, landing soundlessly on the resistant pile of a Turkish rug. I'd felt my fingers becoming clumsy as I covered the pages of the reporter's pad with my erratic script, but more disturbingly, had experienced a growing certainty that someone had appeared behind me, following all I wrote. I couldn't help glancing back whenever O'Garretty hesitated in his speech, but the various elements there were keeping themselves to themselves.

O'Garretty stooped for the pen before I'd had the chance, and I glimpsed again, at the tips of his fingers, a silvery nimbus so fleeting that, afterwards, I couldn't be sure of what I'd seen.

"Everything going all right?" My difficulties, then, were apparent. "I forget my manners. May I offer you a drink? Some tea or coffee? Or something stronger?"

"A glass of water would be good," I said. "Just a little dehydrated, I think."

How thankful I was to be left alone for the few minutes of his absence. I took a few deep breaths and flexed my fingers, adjusting my position to finally take ownership of the chair. What was making me so ill at ease? Wasn't I an old hand with these types of people? Was it the otherness I'd detected, and the strain it appeared for him to speak to me, showing itself, especially, in the prolonged pauses where he seemed to search for words? There was a falsity, a kind of vacancy in his voice, a distracting, carrying quality. And there was something about the room itself, a watchfulness roving the soporific air, settling now on the leaves of the parlour palm, now on the shelf of African fetishes, now about the mouth of the wastepaper bin, whose frayed leather walls recalled, to me, a desiccated carcass. I rubbed my eyes, and a streak swept across, like a vanishing white flame.

"Here you are," O'Garretty had re-entered the room so noiselessly that in my abstracted state I hadn't noticed. He handed me a glass of iced water and, clearly animated by his time away, strode straight over to the bookshelves behind his chair, and began dragging out thick volumes, piling them up in his arms. Their intricately embossed covers, even without knowing their contents, quickened my bibliophile's heart, and I downed my glass of water almost in one as I watched.

"Take them," he said. And he dumped a four volume stack at my feet. "Barr's Magickal journals. *The Book of the Divine Interlocutor. The Adamantine Grimoire* and the rest. I don't want them anymore. Anything you want to know about his practice, his wretched philosophy is there."

I set my glass on the rug and stared, not understanding his change of mood or this sudden, but rather belligerent, act of generosity, and when he flung himself into his chair, I saw a new and fervent challenge in his eyes.

"But I didn't allow you here to talk about that man's powers. I wanted you to know what they did. What they did to us. To myself and my companion."

Although my every fibre yearned towards the stack of books, the uppermost volume of which, I could already see, was embossed with script that bore some resemblance to the Honorian, there was no question of me picking them up and inspecting them now. Not with, it seemed, a revelation pending.

"These days," he said with vehemence, "it would be called grooming." And his hands, which rested on one knee of his crossed legs, tightened so that the knuckles showed white. "But *they*," he continued, "those people, did whatever they liked, justifying any cruelty in the name of the Work. You should know—and don't think I can't see your acquisitive eyes—that there are several pages missing from *The Book of the Divine Interlocutor*. These pages have been destroyed. They described a ritual conducted in an outbuilding of this house. And yes, this house was Barr's. He left it, and considerable wealth, to me, because he had no choice. There was no other place for us to go."

I picked up my pen, but my hand, still chilled by the glass of water, was trembling, and at the same time my fingers slipped as if they'd been sweating in rubber gloves. Was it my imagination, or the newly fevered atmosphere, that made me think the room had brightened? Were they specks of illuminated dust, those minute lucencies, sinking slowly through the air? They might have been, if the day hadn't been so dark. I looked back to the lined page and tried to write the word "grooming", but the pen skidded, leaving an ineloquent black mark. Since I seemed to have temporarily lost the knack of writing, I'd have to remember as best I could whatever O'Garretty had to say about his personal darkness. His companion, he'd said, had been the victim of Barr's cruelty too? I'll admit that I felt out of my depth when it came to allegations of abuse. I would have to take advice, when it came to the book. And should I ask about the companion? Or would I be allowed to speak to them?

"I was a beautiful young man," he began, "although you wouldn't think so now."

I stifled a laugh. But honestly, if this was a man who'd lost his looks, what hope was there for the rest of us?

"People used to say I was like a Greek god. They said I had a charisma that no man or woman could resist. Really, you can't imagine it. But at eighteen I was still a virgin, having developed a disgust for the slobbering, pawing attention I'd received all throughout my adolescence. What others would have seen as an enviable gift, made me feel a freak, isolated and unengaged, and I avoided any kind of closeness and distrusted what anyone else would have seen were blameless overtures of friendship. It was this chasteness, this loneliness, and this physical beauty, that made me perfect for their schemes."

He stopped abruptly, tensing as if at an unexpected sound. And perhaps there was, at the very edge of my hearing, something, there and gone, like the click of a camera lens. O'Garretty's eyes were wide with apprehension, and strangest of all, I could have sworn that their irises, which I knew to be blue, were an almost iridescent green. I was about to ask what had disturbed him when a violent tremor shook his shoulders, his arms, and the hands that gripped his knees.

"O'Garretty ?" I sat forward in alarm. Was this a fit? Epilepsy? "Are you okay?"

He turned towards me, and his poise was restored, and his gaze was calm and clear and blue. "I'm quite well, thank you," he said. "Quite well. Nothing to worry about. Let me go on."

I was far from convinced that O'Garretty was as well as he insisted—he'd had what seemed to be a seizure, after all. But he'd pulled himself together quickly enough, and it wasn't my place to pry. What choice did I have but deference? And if truth be told, I put my concerns aside once he resumed his narrative with a new, unwavering fluency, much as if he'd never had any other tempo.

He could paint quite a picture. I could almost smell the fug of patchouli, canteen food and cigarettes that filled the corridors of Canterbury Art School in 1962, and I could almost see its huddled coteries of beatniks and teenage philosophers, complete with duffle coats and pipes. This was the heady milieu in which he first met Lucia Stanway, then a visiting professor; for she it was who lured the young and pulchritudinous O'Garretty into the heart of Barr's circle. A flamboyant figure, widely revered for her uncanny way with portraiture, Stanway had praised O'Garretty's ability, his talent, in a measured and academic way that both flattered and convinced. And she had, to his pleasure and surprise, also noticed the book by the artist and mage Austin Osman Spare that he'd taken to carrying with him—for like many lonely dreamers, O'Garretty was fascinated by the occult. It was at Stanway's invitation that he first visited Franklin Barr's secluded country house, ostensibly to view his collection of Spare etchings—the oldest trick in the book, but one that a troubled young man was sure to miss.

O'Garretty's eyes returned to the shelf of ancient funerary goods, while, in a embittered tone, he told me how Barr and his twelve followers should really have been on the stage, being such gifted actors, and that the greatest of their theatrical performances had been the pantomime of their art that they'd performed over the course of the following year. He'd grown giddy, swept along, thrilled to learn the secret mantras, which he now knew to be meaningless, and by his first forays into astral travel, and the part he played in solemn, prop-laden rituals, where he directed himself at all times, as they instructed, to be ready, to be worthy, to accept the full power of Angelic Love. They gained his trust, his devotion, and he became intoxicated by his own beauty, seeing it as the miracle they told him it was, and he allowed them to dress him, to anoint him, to cover his naked, unresisting flesh in sigils they drew with their own blood. After a year he eagerly agreed to take part in what they assured him might be their most dangerous and precious rite; a transference of Love between the disincarnate and the fleshed, the materialisation of, and dialogue with, a life form that had already communicated its willingness. But what they'd been doing was not sharing, not involving him, not leading him through the steps of an initiation. All along, they'd been concealing their true intent.

"Can you imagine," O'Garretty said, "how it felt, me, the axis of their circle, naked, burnished, anointed with narcotic perfumes, crowned and flower bedecked, as they performed the rite of which I will not speak? How I felt when, entranced and, at the last moment psychically and physically paralysed, I realised they'd used me as bait? When a being, consumed by, as they'd hoped, love, no, *passion*, for me came into their midst? A being that, like them, knew full well how to deceive. For this being had no intention of communicating any further with *them*. No, it had quite other plans as far as *they* went. They'd been only too successful in drawing its love to me, you see. And now it had me, it wasn't going to let go."

He looked at me with disarming directness, and again I felt as if we were viewing each other across an inconceivable distance, one so vast that there was no way we could ever truly meet. "Do you mean—" I said. I did not, however, finish voicing the suspicion that had risen to my mind; O'Garretty had swayed unsteadily to his feet, eyes frantic, one hand feeling back towards the chair, seeking its support.

"Do you hear that?" he whispered. "Is it audible to you?" But I was, at that moment, unaware of anything except his trembling figure and his extraordinary, anguished look. All I could hear were what may have been the normal small sounds of an old house, a little of the faint clicking I'd heard earlier, before his seizure, only rather slower, and perhaps more regularly paced.

"Well, I...I'm not sure I can hear anything much."

But O'Garretty took no notice of my non-committal reply. "Wait here," he said. "There's something I must see to." He pushed himself away from the chair, and I fully believed, so frail did he appear as he walked to the door, that he was close to physical collapse. But the thud of a heavy fall did not come. I heard only his retreating footsteps and what was, perhaps, the distant turning of a lock.

I gazed towards the garden window, trying to make sense of what was happening, of what O'Garretty had told me, and its implications. But I was seized once again by the sense of being watched, and more precisely that the watcher had just risen from the chair at the desk—the chair that was now turned towards me, when I was sure that it had faced away. It was as if some trace of energy lingered there, as if a process of quietening was not complete, and the skeletal wooden arms were grasping after the someone, or the something, that had abandoned them.

I pushed aside my imaginings, turning to the stack of rare, even unique, books beside my feet. But before my fingers had so much as brushed their pristine covers, I pulled back, afraid I'd be burned by the phosphorescence that had seemed to flare across the finely embossed script. And then the pressure in my bladder, which I'd up till then been ignoring, became an urgent demand. I squeezed myself from my seat and hurried to the entrance hall, hoping that, by a stroke of luck, I'd hit upon the way to a bathroom.

There was a door on my right, which I found to be locked, and, leading from the other side of the entrance hall, past the first stage of the staircase, a narrow length of hallway, with a terminal door and a couple at either side. Now on the edge of desperation, I tried the first on my left, and I gave thanks to whichever gods were listening when I saw the run of old encaustic tiling and the trusty cistern lavatory, complete with hanging chain. I felt lighter, freer, afterwards. I washed my hands at the deep basin, enjoying the honest clank of the pipes and the tarry fragrance of the cracked soap, and I supposed it was a tint in the old mirror glass that lent my face a grey pallor. All mirrors lie, to some extent.

On returning to the narrow hallway, I stood for a moment, all ears. Was he down here, or upstairs? Had he gone in search of medication—pills, or an injection, perhaps? But was that a voice? Yes—I could hear it now, and it was him, speaking in muted tones, close by. I crept towards the final door, stopping at the point where eavesdropping might plausibly be denied. Who was he talking to? His *companion*? And in what language? The rhythm of it, the guttural dissonance, couldn't possibly be English. He paused, as though anticipating a reply. And how could it have been so slight, so ethereal, the response that came, and yet have been as terrifying as the roar of a fighter jet ripping through the sky? It seared through me like red hot wires, piercing my skull in a thousand places, plucking at each nerve as though they were the strings of a delicate, and infinitely strung, instrument of pain

I wasn't aware of blundering into the bare room until the agony, the overwhelming blur of it, subsided. My surroundings, though, seemed unremarkable, although I had the feeling, from the yellowing of the walls, and the accumulation of dust upon the floor, that the space had long been set aside. There were, however, no cobwebs; no sign that spiders, those lovers of neglect, had made it their home, or their grave. The aural torment must have ceased —I wouldn't, I was sure, otherwise so easily escape it. But had the attack come from within me, or without? Had I actually heard anything, or had it been the neurological payback of an over-tired brain? I'd started to turn around when something at the window, just above the tangle of leaves outside, drew my eye. It had the pure fluorescence of a full moon emerging from the darkest sky, and when I turned back, curious, the room had spun itself, from nothing, a storm of crystal lights, dazzling and darkening like the diamond eyes of stars. And the walls themselves, it seemed to me, could only just contain the gleaming flow beneath their skins, their straight lines lost, their corners swelling and slipping from a brilliant, blinding, inner radiance. As I moved back, a universe of astral eyes burned into me, and I knew that what they beheld was, to them, completely insignificant.

All was quiet in the hallway. O'Garretty, I hoped, was still occupied elsewhere, and it was in a detached state that I made my way back to the big room; in a state, you could say, of denial about my mystifying ordeal. What I'd experienced couldn't have been objectively real. More likely, it was the prelude to a particular type of migraine. I'd read about those kinds of things, though never a sufferer myself; the triggers were as unpredictable as the sensory effects. But my departure was to be swift. Franklin Barr's books, and his short biography, had given me everything I'd wanted—in fact, more than I'd hoped—and there was no need for me to impose further upon what I suspected to be a very sick man. This was how I justified my plan to run from what I dared not face. To my relief, the room was empty, and as I gathered the books into my bag, not risking another glance at their covers, I considered whether the politest thing to do would be to leave a thank you note. It was to prove unnecessary, however; a certain drawing-in of the atmosphere told me my host had returned.

"You were exploring?" he said.

I swung around, and perhaps for the only time in my life read the signs of death upon a person who so recently seemed to have escaped the ravages of time.

"No...I mean, I'm sorry if I've intruded in any way. It wasn't my intention, but listen, O'Garretty, do you need me to call a doctor?"

A gaunt asymmetry, a new and shocking corruption, showed in the face before me, so that I wasn't entirely sure how this could be the same person. The mouth, before so sculptural, now drooped at one corner, and his skin seemed to have thinned, pulling hard around the sockets of his eyes, and withering at his cheeks and between his neck and jaw. He leaned against the open door, pressing down upon the handle, so that I worried, at any moment, it would swing and send him sprawling.

"If..." He stopped to swallow painfully. "If you'd be so kind as to help me to my chair."

Letting fall my laden bag, I went to him, and with my arm around his waist, walked him across. I might have been an attentive nephew tending to a beloved uncle, to anyone looking in. But there was more fear than compassion in my voice when, seeing him like that, I asked the question I could no longer avoid.

"Your companion, O'Garretty," I said. "Are they what I think?"

He tried to smile, but this exertion drew new suffering to his sadly altered face. I had to lean in when he'd gathered himself enough to speak, and when he did, it was with a voice that barely rose above a murmur.

"Well, that depends...on what you think. For some while I've known that my companion is dying. Your presence here was...too much for them. This place, the protection Barr gave it, was never meant to last as long as this." His left hand, now clawing inwards, reached out to lightly brush my own.

"We aren't made to be loved by them," he declared between weak breaths. "It is...abominable. We have some of what they are in us...their howling light...their terrible ecstasy...but in us it is less than a single spark. Oh no, don't look so horrified. You won't be affected. You won't be slowly pulled apart from the inside...like Barr and all that circus. No. Not enough left...for that. Or I'd never have... let you come here."

His hand dropped away, and his head fell forward, and a deep shudder passed through him. "I didn't think," he said, with what I feared was a last summoning of strength, "it was so near. Please, you'd better leave. I don't know what will happen. But—" And he looked off into the air, which had taken on, while he was speaking, the same silvery light that danced across his skin. "But I suspect that if anyone looks, they'll find no trace of us."

***

When I left the house I was met by the front garden's vivid life. I stood for a while, gazing at a patch of camellias whose pink blooms had fallen to the grass entire, so they looked like small impractical craft cast adrift. The ground beneath the holly and the laurel was silent, still and dark, and birds were singing, high and invisible to me, and I wondered if I'd ever open Barr's books or leave them untouched, so they'd always be, like his legacy, the stuff of rumour and myth.

Charon
Christian Dickinson

"A penny for the old guy, if you please,
To cross in peace the black and bitter stream
And stand before the Three upon the beam;
Elysium or Tartarus to ease."

He curls his fingers round the obolus
And nods behind him to the narrow boat.
The skiff bobs as you step into the float,
Which soon rejoins the liquid terminus.

He makes no sound upon the lonely mile
As blinding dark extinguishes your sight
(save for the plash of water in the void).
Yet ere you curse the silence unalloyed—
The boards upon the adverse ground alight.
"You may debark," he drones, "You're here awhile."

The Hungry Man
David O'Mahony

"Don't stand on it, Luke, don't stand on it!"

Abbey caught his arm, pulling him off balance so he didn't plant one of his size nine boots on the brown grass.

"What? Huh?" Hauling himself up he was more confused than angry. He had been staring at the trees up ahead and listening to their cacophony of summer birdsong rather than looking where he was going.

Abbey pointed to the lump he had nearly stood on. It was only a few inches higher than the rest of the sweeping lawn but was a morose brown in a sea of fresh green. It was as if the stalks of meadow grass, skeletal quaking-grass, and the handful of dandelions and nettles that had tried to colonise it had been leeched of life and left broken shells of what they aspired to be.

"It's a bump," Luke said. There was no shortage. They were walking through the grounds of Maytown House in Galway, near Ireland's craggy western shore. It had been settled and abandoned and ploughed and replanted a thousand times. There were abandoned shrubberies and flowerbeds all across the land, oases of colonisation reclaimed by the hazels, whitethorns, and soft pink dog-thorns ever since the house and its grounds were abandoned at the height of the great famine, when one in eight people on the island died of hunger or disease.

"It's hungry grass, Luke."

"Sorry, what?"

"Hungry grass. Have you never heard of it?"

Luke was from the heart of suburban Cork City. His heart beat with the throbbing of car engines rather than the lilt of forgotten tales. "No idea what you're on about."

Abbey sighed. She was from Skibbereen in rural Cork County, where they remembered the spectres of starvation. "Hungry grass, it's where somebody died during the famine. Probably just dropped dead and never got buried, or a priest never got to them. My nan used to tell us about it. The Hungry Man, she called it. If you step on the hungry grass you'll get haunted or possessed, that's what she used to say. Won't stop until he gets his fill."

"Oh, not this shit again." Luke made an indelicate sound. They had some things in common, but unlike Abbey he had no patience for the supernatural, and despite her pleas to leave her alone in what she believed he had needled her over it to the point where he was on the verge of breaking things off with her after two years. He had planned this as a last-ditch effort to see if there was a future together.

"Christ, you know what I think of this rubbish."

"Look, can you not just do one thing for me? Literally just one thing? You've been such an ass the past few months. This is important to me," she said.

He stomped on the brown mound, driving his heels into it. "Look, nothing's happening." He spread his hands wide and did a mocking little dance. "No ghost, no zombie, nothing."

Abbey balled up her fists and narrowed her eyes. Her nostrils flared and closed and flared again. Luke realised suddenly that she had come on the trip for the same reasons he had, to see if there was anything worth saving. She was wound tight and ready to snap. Just being around him was causing her physical pain. "Forget about it. It's like being with a toddler. Let's just go back to the camp."

Luke sighed but she was already on the move, her long legs opening a distance between them that he could not close.

They were staying in a small tourist cottage on the edge of a manmade lake. There were six little buildings arranged in a semicircle near a jetty that lords and ladies had used to launch their boats for a summer afternoon's row or dalliance. Now it had benches and a fire pit and was used for drinking parties. It was early in the season; they were the only guests.

Abbey barely spoke to Luke for the afternoon, preferring to sit under a tree with her books and earbuds. Luke sat on a bench, eating roasted peanuts from a plastic container and thinking about jumping in the car and leaving. But it wasn't his car. So they sat apart, getting used to no longer being in one another's existence.

Dusk came and went. Abbey ate cold shredded chicken with cheese and chili at the table. It was leftovers from the restaurant they'd stopped at in Limerick, a meal shared with so much strained silence they should have turned around. They had kept going, mostly out of stubbornness.

Watching Abbey, facing away from him, Luke's stomach complained but he couldn't face going inside until he saw her close the door to the bedroom. He grabbed a block of cheese from the fridge and sliced bread from a cupboard but he could barely taste the sandwich. And no matter how much he ate the hunger pains just didn't go away. Throwing the crusts onto the countertop, he took a bottle of mature whiskey – a welcoming gift from the camp owners – and grabbed a blanket from the three-seater leather couch before going back out into the night, flicking off the lights but leaving the door ajar so he didn't get locked out. The night was still and empty without even the hum of an insect to keep him company.

Prying the cap off and dumping himself back onto the wooden bench he wondered how anybody could find this relaxing. A vast wheel of glimmering stars circled over him, punches of light in the black blanket of the night sky. The near silence was claustrophobic. The hint of a breeze ruffled the grass and in the distance a fox barked. Give him the rumble of traffic and random shouts of drunkards in the distance over this any day. At least he would feel a part of life, not exiled in the quiet of the countryside.

He winced at the taste of the whiskey, then spat it out. It had neither spice nor bite; it was like burnt dust mixed with water. He dropped the bottle and listened to it heave into the gravel. Slumping forward with his head in his hands, he almost didn't hear the crunch of a foot on stone behind him.

"Abbey?"

The crunch came again, followed by the slide of somebody coming to a halt.

He turned, flicking on his phone's pitiful white torch but the thing was on him almost before he saw it.

Middling height and shirtless, the man's papery skin was stretched tight across his ribs and shoulders. Mottled and blue he lumbered toward Luke with effort, scattering the gravel as he tried to raise a small cup in front of him, rocking it so a lonely coin scraped the bottom; his twig-like arms seemed to lack the strength to hold it up. His hair was missing in patches and covered in soil. He opened his mouth as if begging for help; most of his teeth were missing and his gums had shrivelled.

Luke stumbled backwards but had nowhere to go. He crashed into the bench and rolled onto the ground, yelping. The man kept coming. His trousers were rotten, ragged things and his feet were black with dirt and decay. And yet still he kept coming, the pathetic little wooden bowl in front of him and the lips soundlessly working until it coughed out "Help, sir. I'm hungry, sir". Luke's nostrils filled with the scent of sweet damp earth, fetid flesh, and desperation as the man loomed over him. As he bore down Luke saw the skin was peeling from his face, showing scrapings of hard white bone. The man's breath stank of bile, fermented grass, and sulphur. Night gathered and swept Luke away.

***

Something was hitting him in the ribs. Opening his eyes, growling at being blinded by the sun, he rolled away from the jabbing.

"Come on. Get up, you tool. Christ's sake." Abbey was over him, prodding him firmly in the ribs with a hiking boot. "Passing out drinking like you're still sixteen. My mother was right about you. I should've seen it ages ago." He heard the empty whiskey bottle clatter as she kicked it out of the way and it went rolling toward the lake. "We're going home."

He had never seen Abbey this angry and the thought of being in the car with her for three hours back to Cork was daunting. "I'm dropping you at the train station in Galway. If you're not ready in ten minutes I'm going without you." She sniffed the air. "Jesus you stink. Were you rolling in the mud or something? Christ. At least have a shower before you get in the car."

She turned and strode in one fluid movement. The car door was already open and as he brushed rough stones from his clothes Luke saw her bags were already in the boot.

Maybe we always knew it wouldn't turn into something serious, he thought. She had started going out with him in part to spite her mother, he knew that; her mother was a hard woman, deeply Catholic with aristocratic tastes and Abbey had made a beeline for the first working-class atheist she could find once she moved to the city for college. He had teased her for her accent, her mannerisms. At first she'd taken it as playful sparring and given as good as she got with his city accent and rough edges, but as the months turned to years both of their joshing had taken a harder edge. And he'd always done little things – like leaving the cap off the toothpaste – simply to annoy her, not thinking but perhaps hoping it would be cumulative. Even the stoutest dam will break if under enough pressure at one point.

He was startled out of reverie by the car horn blaring. His stomach ached but the fridge and cupboards were empty bar a box of teabags. He wandered into the bathroom – his bags and toiletries were still in the cabin – and turned on the shower. It wasn't that far to the train station, he thought, he could eat then. Stepping in and closing his eyes, he let the water pummel him in the hope it would shake out some of the tension across his neck and chest.

As he squeezed shampoo into his hand he thought he saw a shadow move behind him. "Abbey?" he called.

Turning around he saw the face of the man pressed against the shower door, his skin flaking away even more than the night before. His lips had begun to peel away, leaving a perpetual snarl on one side and ruined teeth poking through. His eyes were milk-white and sunk deep into his skull. The stink of death hit Luke like a wave and he retched, but his stomach was too empty to bring anything up. The man tapped a bowl against the glass quietly, insistently, his mouth struggling to form the words "I'm hungry" over and over.

Luke screamed and smacked the back of his head against the tiled wall, scrunching his eyes tight in pain and terror. When his eyes opened the dead man was gone. "Losing my mind," he snapped at himself, turning off the water. "Losing it."

Drying himself only enough to stop his clothes from being damp he hurled everything he had brought into his battered plastic case and powered his way out of the cabin as fast as he could. The key was on the kitchen table.

Throwing his case into the boot on the way, he dropped heavily into the passenger seat. Abbey eyed him up warily. "You're pale," she said eventually. "Are you sick? Because I'm not driving you if you're going to throw up all over my mother's car."

"No, not sick," he muttered.

As she twitched her lips he knew she was asking herself what she'd ever seen in him to begin with, and even in his own head he couldn't come up with an answer. She started the car and they trundled softly over the gravel. Luke closed his eyes. His stomach was turning and he felt flushed. "Can I turn on the air? I need some air." The vents huffed into life but the cold only took the edge off. He sat back and hoped for sleep.

It was nearly ten minutes before they made it to something resembling a main road, ten minutes without even a note of music to break the silence. Not that Luke made an effort. He was content to lose himself in the rumble of wheels on gravel until it gave way to the smooth flow of asphalt and he could slip away into unconsciousness.

He missed what Abbey was saying.

"Sorry, what?" he asked.

She blew air through pursed lips. "I said, you'll need to get your few bits out of my flat."

"Oh. Yeah." There wasn't much. A toothbrush, a few changes of clothes, a few books he wouldn't miss. It would be almost as if he'd never been there, he thought, thinking over his own apartment and realising slowly that she had left nothing he could remember.

"Wait, what the hell is that?" he shouted, heart freezing. A skeletal man in a ragged, mud-caked blanket was walking next to the road. Abbey braked, and as she did they pulled right next to him. A cavernous rotten face turned slowly to peer in the window at Luke as it mouthed "I'm hungry".

Luke screamed and tried to throw himself away from the window, knocking against Abbey and sending the car veering into the ditch on the far side of the road, with only the fact they had already slowed saving them from ploughing into a pile of broken rock overhung by angry trees. The car lurched slightly as the engine stalled. Had it been spring or autumn the ground would have been damp and the wheels would have burrowed into the mud, but it was a fine summer's day and the ground was dusty and hard.

"What the hell is wrong with you?" Abbey shouted, unbuckling and freeing herself from the car in one move. Luke reached out to her. "Jesus Christ! You're a psychopath," she said. "Get your hands away from me."

"I got a fright–"

"From what?"

"The man on the road."

Abbey threw both hands in front of her and gestured up the road and then down it. It was empty apart from a little black crow sitting in the middle of the asphalt. "Who? WHO? I just... I can't do this any more. I thought I could at least do this drive but I can't even look at you. Get out."

"What?"

"I said get out of the damn car!"

Unbuckling, he peeled himself off the seat and out the door, testing the ground to make sure he didn't sink. "Where am I going to go?"

Abbey was already opening the boot. "You know what? I actually don't care," she said, then paused with her hand on the lid. "I actually don't care," she said again, almost whispering to herself like a revelation. "Two years wasted. You're a grown man. You have legs. The road only goes one place. Figure something out."

She dropped his case into the ditch and swung her door shut harder than she meant to. The engine thunked and growled for a few seconds before erupting into life, and she had floored the pedal and begun reversing almost before Luke had a chance to get out of the way.

The car paused on the road for a second, Abbey looking resolutely ahead before pulling it into gear and taking off without looking back.

Running his hands through his hair, Luke swore, as much at himself as her. As he picked the case up by the handle he heard the faint clink of a coin in a pewter cup.

The hair on his nape standing on end, he swallowed hard as his nostrils filled with the smell of damp peat and decay. He turned to find the dead man barely a step away, shaking his alms cup with one hand even as his other, shorn of flesh and now just blackened muscle and bone, clamped down on Luke's shoulder, the broken yellowed nails tearing easily through his clothes and right into the meat. Luke cried out and pulled away as cold agony pulsed down his arm and torso. "I'm hungry, sir," the dead man said, as if recovering some of his strength. "Help me."

Throwing the case between them Luke took off toward the woods, scrabbling over the ditch and almost falling as he plunged into the treeline without any plan apart from running on as fast as he could for as long as he could.

A chill ran along his spine from the wound in his shoulder, a chill that whispered he had been marked for death and his fate was inevitable. He hated her for throwing him out of the car, if only because he didn't want to die alone. His lungs screamed and his legs burned. How long had he been running? Hours? But he looked back to find he could still see the road some way in the distance, at the end of a slope he hadn't realised he was climbing.

Through the woods the faint sound of the alms cup followed him, seeming to come from the trees up ahead one moment and then far behind him. The dead man's voice called to him, earnest and growing stronger.

Looking back to try and spot the man Luke tripped and stumbled out of the trees and onto an exposed hillside. It was ribboned with dry stone walls and veined with row upon row of rough earthen mounds that reminded him of tiny barrow graves. A handful of pitiful foundations were all that remained of cottages abandoned at the height of the famine. The hillside was blasted and fallow, so dogged and rough that nobody would ever think of it as having been homes for families who had endured out of a stubbornness rooted in the earth itself. Much of the ground was stripped bare by wind and neglect, with clumps of sodden meadow grass holding the soil together in a fevered embrace. Luke rose and fell with the mounds of the landscape. The bumps and raises in the soil were the legacy of elder times, the remnants of potato lazy beds that had fed legions until the black days when their promise and strength gave out and the legions fell alongside them.

The ring of a coin in the alms cup echoed across the landscape, filling his ears like the thunder of a cathedral's bell. Luke clambered over the lazy beds, vaguely hoping that if he could get to the top of the hill he might be able to spot help, or at the very least civilisation. Clouds drifted in front of the sun like God averting his gaze.

Panting hard, Luke misplaced a step at the top of a lazy bed and fell like a dying oak onto the ground, crying out as something cracked in his ankle.

The clouds broke and he was blinded by a spear of sunshine. Whimpering, he tried to pull himself to his feet but collapsed in agony as his ankle refused to support his weight. The clink of the alms cup came ever closer.

"I'm hungry," said the man, his voice hammering in Luke's brain. "Help me, sir. I'm hungry."

A shadow loomed over Luke, blotting out the sun. A haggard corpse, eating itself as the skin peeled away. "Please, sir. I'm hungry."

Dragging himself backward with his hands, Luke cried out as an unnaturally heavy foot stomped down on his wounded leg, driving it into the dirt. "I'm hungry, sir. I'm hungry," the voice said, coming from all around now as the shadow-shrouded corpse didn't descend, but melted down on top of him.

Luke screamed as he felt the skin peeling off his bones

from the legs up. The dead man's face began to plump up, ever so slowly, as it ravenously devoured every muscle and sinew. Luke began to descend into the earth as if the ground itself was opening to welcome him home.

"I'm hungry, sir," the creature said, its voice thickening as it plunged its hand into Luke's chest, breaking apart the ribs to expose the heart. Luke, hovering on the edge of death, was beyond feeling pain even as the creature placed the alms cup inside him. Then it placed both hands kindly on Luke's temples, as gently as if he were a newborn, and as Luke slipped into the blackness of the grave, feeling the brown hungry grass blossoming over and out of his body, he saw his own face staring back at him as his own voice whispered "thank you, sir".

Will-o'-the-Wisp
Sarah Cannavo

Weary traveler, take care where you tread
if o'er the moors by night you choose to stray,
seeking a shortcut home to your warm bed.
Weary traveler, take care not to tread
where the blue flames flicker, lest you be led
deep into the dark marsh, ne'er to see day.
Weary traveler, take care where you tread
if o'er the moors by night you choose to stray.

Something Lost
Gregory Meece

The stone was real. I held it twice—at the bookends of my life. But was *she* real? Or has my advanced age made me addle-brained, as my doctors believe? Has time fused the fragments of my memories into a narrative based on what never occurred? As a child, my parents would have chalked it up to an overactive imagination, which, unlike my corporeal condition, remains intact.

There is a third possibility, though neither logic nor reason can support it. My time in this world is short, but I will use what little remains of it to share my story. You are free to decide whether it's a symptom of an old man's mental decline, a product of a ripe imagination, or, as I believe, something that truly happened.

I begin with the incident that occurred when I was ten years old. They say many people of my vintage can remember distant events vividly yet forget where they placed their eyeglasses just moments earlier. Psychologists believe this may relate to how early life events are often tied to formative emotional milestones. In my case, that's certainly the case.

***

"That Theodore. He sure has some imagination."

Although I took my parents' words to mean silly, childish—one who acts immaturely, I didn't let it bother me. I could always lock my bedroom door and take out my army men to stage history's greatest battle. Or I could read my Superman comic books for the hundredth time. Without imagination, how could the people who wrote them know what Planet Krypton or Metropolis looked like?

When I needed a greater distance from home to be alone with my thoughts, I would visit the creek. It was only a few blocks, but the journey was charged with anticipation. Adventure awaited me in the woods, fringed with its giant oak, wild cherry, and ghostly sycamore trees —a fertile spot for young imaginations to thrive.

One summer day, I ventured deeper to explore an area

just beyond an outcropping of rocks where the creek bent. On the opposite side, the water was still and deep—a good place to dangle a fishing line. On the inside bank, the water flowed quickly over a bed of small stones.

The stream was gentle enough to wade across in my pursuit of crayfish lurking beneath smooth stones. The sun's glare across the rippled surface disguised the streambed. I bent forward, scanning the water, like a heron looking to spear its next meal. Patient, yet anxious, I waded against the current, my eyes focused, hoping to spot minnows or tadpoles darting among the tiny caves formed by the rocks.

After a few minutes, an object caught my eye—a stone with a pinkish-grey hue. It was its shape, however, rather than its colors, which separated it from the thousands of other stones. What the others had in common was just that—they were common. Their irregularity was what made them indistinguishable. This stone stood out because of its symmetry. I reached into the cool stream and raised the object. Two or three inches long and less than an inch wide, the stone was tapered to a point on one end.

An arrowhead! The best thing a boy could ever hope to find—a hundred times better than a four-leaf clover. The only experience close to what I felt was Christmas morning, when weeks of eager anticipation were rewarded with the first magical glimpse of presents beneath the tree. But those gifts were meant to be found. This discovery had been hidden for hundreds of years. It might easily have stayed that way forever. That's why it was so special—a tangible echo of a distant past, now cradled in my hands.

The hollow bubbling sound of water lapping against the rocks distracted me, so, at first, I didn't notice the arrival of the two boys. When I looked up, I recognized them from school. They were in the higher grades. We didn't ride the same bus, which was good because I'd heard they liked to bully younger kids.

"Hey, what you lookin' at?" the taller, red-haired boy asked, his voice more confrontational than curious. He was shirtless, which somehow made him appear more menacing.

"It's an arrowhead," I said. "Found it." Something told me to tone down my excitement.

"That ain't a real arrowhead. Let me see it," the red-haired boy challenged me.

I had little choice in the matter, so I waded to the bank and handed the arrowhead up to him. "See the notches?" I showed him. "That's how Indians attached them to their arrows. Probably Lenapes."

"Probably what?" he asked. He ought to have said 'who,' but I wasn't inclined to correct him.

"The Lenape Indians lived here a long time ago. They used bows and arrows to hunt. I read about them in a library book."

"Well, ain't you a little know-it-all?" the boy sneered. I could have added that the stone was quartzite, but that would not have helped my situation.

Fingering my arrowhead, the boy rubbed its edges, as if checking to see if it was still sharp enough to kill something. "Sounds like he's some kind of expert," the other boy said. He was not as big as the red-haired boy, but he looked tough because of the way he stood—like one of the thugs in *Dick Tracy*. I knew by the way he said "expert" that it was meant to mock me.

Suddenly, the red-haired boy reared his arm like he was going to pitch a fastball. He sailed my arrowhead deep into the overgrown brush where he knew it would be impossible for me to retrieve it. The henchman boy patted the other's shoulder as if he'd just won a prize. They paraded down the path, into the woods. With my eyes filling with liquid, the pair were a blur. Their hooting and cackling slowly faded as the breeze mercifully carried the cruel sounds away. Then, all that was left was the complicit laughter of the water's murmuring rush.

The next day, I returned to the stream and located the exact spot on the shore where the red-haired boy stood when he launched my arrowhead. I recreated its trajectory and aimed toward where I thought it might have landed. Soon, however, the vegetation became so thick and thorny that it was impossible to move forward. Robust poison ivy vines covered the ground and snaked up the sides of trees. The chances were high that I was going to leave there with deep cuts and scratches, a bad rash, and no arrowhead, so I turned back.

"Hi. What are you doing?"

It was a girl's voice, gentle and sweet. I spun around and saw her standing in the water, with the bubbles forming rings around her ankles. She looked like she was about my age. Her smiling face, caught by a ray of sunshine, seemed to reflect its brilliance. Tied in her hair was a cornflower blue ribbon—a delicate slice trimmed from the sky. I couldn't turn away.

"I was just looking for something," I said. "I think I lost it here yesterday."

"What was it? Maybe I can help find it."

"I don't think so. Probably gone forever. It's okay though. What's your name?"

"It's Dori. Dori Jacobs. Well, Dorothy, really. *Wizard of Oz* is my parents' favorite movie, but I'm me—just 'Dori.'"

"I'm just Theo," I said as I plucked a flat, smooth stone from the ground and sent it skimming across the stream's deep end. Dori watched, wide-eyed, as if I had just performed an impossible feat of magic. I knew that someone had because, suddenly, everything seemed right again.

I showed Dori how to pick out the best stones for skipping and how to hold them between her fingers to make a sidearm throw. She held her hand over her mouth to stifle a giggle when her stone landed "splat" in the water. We both laughed, filling the woods with happiness as flashes of light glinted off the water that danced around our bare feet. That was the best day I ever had.

I forgot about my lost arrowhead until Dori brought it up. "Tell me again what you lost?" she said. We sat together on a lichen-covered log, our toes dangling in the water. We were so comfortable talking, playing, pretending. There was no risk of embarrassment or shame. When I related the episode of the pair of bullies who cost me my greatest find, I knew she would understand how I felt. And that made everything better.

We departed our wooded playground and continued to talk with an intimacy usually reserved for long-time friends. Without the slightest embarrassment, I even told her how I once tied a sheet across my back and pretended to soar across the neighborhood like Superman. She told me she had a fairy house in her backyard at the base of an old Osage orange tree. The tangled roots created a cavity big enough for the fairies to have a home with a kitchen, a fireplace for cooking, and a bedroom with bookshelves filled with stories of mythological creatures called humans. She peeled the orange bark from the tree and called it "gold." She planned to use some of the gold to pay the fairies to use their magic to locate my arrowhead and return it to me. I felt like I hit a baseball to the moon.

When I reached my street, Dori and I said our goodbyes. The last thing she promised was that she would find a way to recover my lost treasure—the arrowhead. As I watched her walk away, I kept stealing glances over my shoulder, wanting to hold her image in my mind for as long as possible.

I just assumed Dori was new to the neighborhood. With the military base being the biggest thing in our town, families were constantly coming and going. I expected to see her in school—it was almost certain, given that our town had only one elementary school. It didn't occur to me that we would never again play by the stream or share new adventures together.

Normally, I didn't look forward to going to school, but when Monday morning came, I couldn't wait. First thing, I would find Dori. Even if we couldn't talk to each other, just knowing she was there would make my day.

Since I didn't see Dori in my class, the next best thing would have been to spot her during recess. I quickly finished my sandwich and headed outside.

The teachers took turns monitoring recess, keeping the boys on one side and the girls on the other. At that time, it was taboo for boys to cross over or even come within cootie-catching distance of the girls. The vice principal patrolled the edge of the girls' side. I needed to ask her about the new girl, Dori Jacobs, so I sauntered over, careful not to draw undue attention. She informed me that the school hadn't enrolled any new students lately and that she wasn't aware of a child by that name. Then, she simply pivoted away, her attention returning to the hopscotch game as if those chalk-drawn squares were more important.

Then, like an exploding shell, my teacher's voice blasted my thoughts into fragments.

"Earth to Mister Dotson!" she shouted in a condescending tone. "Time to get your head out of those clouds."

Reluctantly, I took my place in the line and followed the other boys.

I wasn't sure what to think. I tried to figure out another way to contact Dori. She must have lived nearby since she walked home from the creek. But I never saw Dori again or heard from anyone who might have known her. I was forced to carry on with my life, going to school, riding my bike, and doing all the things expected of a ten-year-old boy. But I didn't return to the stream. In quiet moments, my thoughts would drift back to when Dori and I skimmed stones over the water's surface. I envisioned us as forever best friends. That's how I dreamed it to be.

***

These memories have lived within me for seventy-five years, but nothing has revived them quite like the strange development I am about to relate.

At the age of eighty-five, I became a "guest" (as they call us) in this assisted living facility—a term that carries its own weight of irony. Holy Saints Assisted Living is where I am to die.

A small sign bearing my name, Theodore Dotson, clings to my door with Velcro, convenient, considering the transient nature of the residents. Recently, a new neighbor moved into 319. I'm 317. I planned to say hello to her, but getting out of bed takes a Herculean effort since I broke my hip. One must factor in the risk-reward ratio for each trip.

The walls are thin, and my in-and-out slumber was interrupted by a sound coming from my neighbor's room.

It was more akin to a whimper than a sob, but I could tell something was wrong. I discerned the words, "Come to me," amidst her sniffles and gasps. Others must have heard her too, I reasoned, but apparently not, because her pleading continued. It was as if she was calling out to me.

Why doesn't she ring for the nurse? I thought. There was always someone on call. Maybe her phone hadn't been hooked up. I reached across my nightstand and pulled the receiver toward me, pressing "1" for the front desk. When the concierge answered, I told her that the woman in the next apartment needed assistance. Could she send someone up? Having fulfilled my neighborly duty, I let my head sink into the pillow, closed my eyes, and swiftly fell back into sleep.

I seldom kept track of time, so I didn't know how long I had been napping. What's the point of measuring the passage of hours when you're in bed all day? When I awoke, I remembered the woman calling from next door. I listened for footsteps or voices in the hallway. All was quiet. Then, I heard her plaintive, "Come to me," once more, followed by soft sighing sounds. Was she having a health-related event or just a bad dream? That happens a lot here. Since we have so much time to rest, so many thoughts clutter our minds.

She needed help, but what could I do? At eighty-five, and with a hip mending, I could barely get out of bed without using someone as my spotter.

I called out, but my voice didn't have enough vigor to leave the apartment. Carefully shifting my weight toward the edge of the bed, I reached for the nightstand for balance. A sharp, clear clatter of breaking glass stopped my progress. I had accidentally knocked over the glass of water I kept by my bed.

Pulling myself up until I could swing my legs over the side of the bed, I reached for my walker. Clasping its cold metal handle, I pulled myself into a standing position. A lance-like pain shot from my hip downward. My posture resembled a question mark, but I was upright, nonetheless.

The floors are tiled to make it easier to push a walker

on a hard surface. Also, it's easier for the cleaning crew to deal with the messes we old people make. After another balance check, I put one foot before the other. When I reached my door, I undid the latch and pushed. A wide turn, then toward the room where I had heard my neighbor's calls. I listened carefully.

Her door was not locked so I pushed it open with my right hand. Before I knew what was happening, my weight shifted. The laws of physics were aptly demonstrated when the wheels of my walker took off in an equal and opposite direction. I heard the clank of aluminum slamming against the steel door jamb as I tried to brace myself. I screamed in pain and crumpled to the floor.

Instinctively, I checked to see if any body parts were in anatomically incorrect positions. I inventoried my bones, hoping not to discover new cracks. Someone was rushing down the hallway. I heard a man shout, "Don't try to get up!" It was not difficult to comply with his command. I could no more get up at that moment than I could dance the polka.

In a few minutes, another helper arrived with a wheelchair. After checking to make sure I could be lifted without causing further damage, the man put his hands beneath my armpits and put me in the chair. Before they rolled me back to my room, I peered into my neighbor's apartment. With everything that had just happened, I almost forgot about why I had left.

The linens and pillow had been removed from the woman's bed. The tops of the nightstand and dresser were empty. As they turned my wheelchair, my eyes took a wider sweep of the room. Nothing. But at the last second, I caught a glimpse of something on the floor, under a corner table where housekeeping must have missed it. The object had a pinkish-grey hue, and it was tapered at one end. I recognized it immediately, though it had been missing for three-quarters of a century. Its reappearance caused my heart to beat faster. I thought, "Could this really be?"

The nurse's voice startled me. "You need to be more careful, Mr. Dotson," she chided, her tone reminiscent of my mother's scoldings. "A broken hip requires bed rest, not another fall." This was hardly breaking news. "You're lucky to have come away with just bruises. Why were you up? Next time, ring for help."

"I did call," I replied. "Nobody came."

"Well, it's good we heard you fall. Your walker might need adjustments. I'll have someone check it."

"What happened to the woman in the next apartment?" I asked.

"I believe our last resident in 319 was a man—a Mr. Thorndike."

"I heard a woman sighing. She was calling ... for me, I think."

"I don't *believe* so," she said, slowly dragging out the word "believe." It was a not-so-subtle way to imply that either an atrophied mind or the effects of medication caused me to be confused. To confirm this, her next sentence was, "Let's get you some rest now."

"Can you at least look on the apartment floor, under the table in the corner? Please, just bring it to me—the stone. I know I saw it there."

She acquiesced and left my apartment. Shortly, she reappeared, sporting a look of disappointment. "I'm so sorry, but I couldn't find anything," she said. She snugly arranged the covers around my neck. It's an old person's version of the pat on the child's head.

Someone from housekeeping popped her head into my room. "I cleaned up his mess and put a new glass of water on the nightstand," she said. On her way out, I could hear the nurse mumble, "We should let the doctor know."

In my youth, it was "silly," "childish," and "imaginative." Now, it has become "senile," "Alzheimer's," and "crazy old man." Yet I knew what I saw; even though my eyes sometimes fail me, my heart assured me it was there. The dream I've carried for so long—the hope of seeing Dori again—That was there, too.

***

A year had passed since my hip healed. Unfortunately, in the category of "If it ain't one thing, it's another," I got something worse. The doctors told me they did all they could do. Having consulted medical professionals for eight decades, I had concluded that "all they can do" is a sliding scale, depending on your time left among the living. Nevertheless, I accepted my prognosis. What would be the point of shooting for a chance at a ninth decade?

Though my days at Holy Saints were numbered, I never expected a visit from Father Rafael, the parish priest. I hadn't stepped foot in a church in decades.

"Holy Saints informs the area parishes of their Catholic residents," Father Rafael said. "Sometimes the residents' families and friends contact us as well. As you know, Mr. Dotson, part of the Church's ministry is to visit and comfort the afflicted. These are part of our Corporal and Spiritual Works of Mercy."

"Wasn't Rafael one of the angels?" I asked.

"Rafael is never named in the Bible," he informed me. "The name comes from Hebrew origins. It means 'God has healed,'"

"Well, the doctors tell me that there's no cure for what ails me."

"Curing is not the same as healing."

"So, why are you here? Extreme Unction?"

"The Church doesn't use that term for the sacrament anymore. We prefer 'Anointing of the Sick.'"

"They don't call this a 'rest home' anymore either."

Father Rafael laughed. He was starting to grow on me.

"I can give you an anointing if that's what you would like me to do," he said. "But that's not the reason I came to see you. I have something to pass on to you."

"Father, never say 'pass on' in a place like this," I joked. He laughed again. I liked him even more.

"It happened after I finished saying Mass," he said. "Typically, I stand outside the church and greet my parishioners as they depart. After everyone left, I went inside and walked toward the sacristy to put away my vestments. On the way, I noticed someone still seated at the end of one of the pews. I assumed she was praying, so I didn't disturb her. When I returned, I planned to ask her if there was something I could do for her, but she was no longer there. I scanned the rest of the church, but it was empty. When I looked at the pew where the woman had been praying, I noticed a small box. There was a note on top. It read, 'Please Deliver: Theodore Dotson, Holy Saints Assisted Living."

Father Rafael reached into his shirt pocket and took out a rectangular box, tied with a cornflower blue ribbon. He moved to the side of my bed and gently placed it in my hand. After Father left, I untied the ribbon and examined the contents of the box.

Inside was what I initially thought was orange tissue paper. Upon closer examination, however, it resembled tree bark. Slowly, I began to unwrap the object inside. It was the arrowhead!

Had she come returned? Was it her voice that I heard, beckoning me to come—my neighbor in 319? Had the fairies worked their magic? Maybe the doctors and nurses were right: my memories were just a jumble, my mind muddled by medicines, old age, and an overactive imagination. Yet, despite the doubts, I gripped the stone so tightly that its sharp edges cut into my hand.

After Father Rafael left, I asked the woman at the front desk if she could check her records to see if anyone named Dorothy Jacobs had ever been a resident at Holy Saints Assisted Living. I suggested she pay particular attention to a year ago. She said she would be happy to check.

Later that afternoon, the phone beside my bed rang. It was the woman I had spoken to earlier.

"Mr. Dotson, I couldn't find anyone by that name in the last couple of years. I did find one guest with the first name Dorothy, but her last name is different."

She changed her name, I thought. "Can you tell me what room she occupied and when she... left?"

"I don't see any harm, considering it was so long ago. Dorothy—she signed 'Dori' in the register—was a guest at Holy Saints Assisted Living a few years back. Unfortunately, she passed away during her stay, just around the time you came to live with us. She was in room 319."

Dori returned to me, as I always believed she would. You may call me a fool or a crazy old man if you must—I won't hold it against you. But I stand firm in my truth: soon Dori and I will be reunited. It's as real as the stone I clutch in my wrinkled hand. Our time together in this life was brief—no more than a summer afternoon. Yet that, I know, was only the beginning of our journey together.

FATE

Billowing castles of airborne dust,
Rolling vistas of heavens,
Night-blown beings of the loveless lust,
Comp'ny the beast in soaring.

And only 'mongst them, through them
Might Unicorn find inner peace.
By regarding reflections from prisms
Find the key to final release.

But some force irresistibly draws it
Deeper within the Light's shadow,
Til it knows that the feeling within it
Do nothing to lift it enow.

And weeping won't stop this, halt this;
A headlong descent into life,
Nor snarling disgust at the kisses,
Those meaningless meaning too rife

    With the empty despair.

Nature's Chandelier by Sonali Roy

The Priest of Hvalsey
K. T. Booker

I've always loved the snow. When I was just a boy, I read of Christian the Fourth and his expeditions to Greenland, to those ancient Norse towns that were said to have disappeared so long ago. At night, in my little room overlooking Copenhagen, I poured over those books. And I guess I fell in love with the Arctic, because I soon decided I'd work my way onto an expedition any way I could.

And I did just that.

I took a contract, at the age of nineteen, on the Danish expedition led by Haeg Redford, or H.R. as we'd call him back then. A two year expedition to make further advances in Arctic sciences. Meteorological, geological, cartography, things such as that. I signed up as an assistant to the meteorologist. A big, jolly man named Lund. I'd fly the weather balloons, store and maintain the equipment. But I became much more than that. I went with some of the boys and learned how to sled on the ice pack and how to hunt the sparse game that presented itself. I was young, foolish with energy, and I tried to make myself as valuable as I could. Because of that, I made on well with the crew.

I can say, truthfully, I loved that trip. I loved the sea and being out and away from Copenhagen. And what I loved most of all was the Arctic. There's nothing like it. I'd have done it for the rest of my life. That is, if what befell me didn't happen.

It was in November of the expedition's second year. Lund wanted to set up a station further up along the coast, to get some more records on the winter weather and atmospherics. But Lund had broken his arm earlier in the summer on a previous sled trip, so I was to go in his stead, seeing as I was pretty familiar with the equipment at that point. Three sleds, six dogs a piece, that was all we could spare at the camp. The Greenlanders, Alfred and Jørgen, went with me. They were experienced sledders and knew how to handle themselves. There's a lot that can go wrong out on the ice, so it was good to know they would be around. I was also riding with Ace as my lead dog. He was Lund's pride and joy and known in the camp as the fiercest pack leader. Lund paid a hefty price for Ace in Nuuk. Him sending Ace with me was a sign of how far our relationship had grown over that year and a half.

Like I said, we set out in early November and the weather was fine. Those first few nights we stayed up on the glaciers, riding by the light of the moon, since the days were getting shorter and shorter. The dogs enjoyed being out in the open air after being housed in the kennel for the previous month.

Those dogs—they are the soldiers of the ice. Tireless. Beautifully shaped for that terrain. It's as if there is nothing more satisfying in the world for them than pulling that sled. At least when they have energy for it. After a few days, when they've tired, you must coax them one way or another. And all the dogs are different, you know. They may act like machines sometimes, but they're just as individual as you and I.

Naturally, there would grow large distances between us. But we were all skilled sledders at this point and understood our way fair enough. At certain distances, we would wait for all to catch up, then we would assemble camp for the night. While I ate and warmed myself with coffee, I'd listen to the stories of Alfred and Jørgen until I dozed off. When I'd wake, those two would already be ready to go, the dogs tied up and howling, pulling on the leashes.

We made good heading those first few days. But the Greenlanders knew our swift progress wouldn't last. And they were right. It was about the sixth day when things started to turn. Our path along the glacier had become more and more uncertain. The cracks could drop you instantly twenty-five meters straight down into an ice gulley. You'd ride right up to these splinters big as a valley and not even know it. We had a few close calls before we finally decided to make our way over the fjords and out onto the coastal ice. It was safer out there. Frozen fairly solid. Though it still could be mighty thin at points. At any rate, it was the better of the two options, regardless of how it turned out for me.

We stopped at intervals and checked the thickness of the ice with a knife. In the thin parts you'd make sure to spread your weight out wide and not move at all as that could lead to a fracture. Even with all the danger out there on the sheet, it was astonishingly beautiful. Some nights you could see the marine life below you all glowing wonderful and pulsing, rhythmic, like some strange form of language. Yet there's an odd feeling in witnessing something like that at night, when you are all alone, and it's so beautiful you have a hard time thinking it's real.

Other times it isn't so magical. That sixth night was like that. The clouds had gathered and dropped down heavy. The moon was gone behind them. I remember it being one of those dreary nights with a curtain of grey mist out in front. You couldn't see more than twenty meters ahead of you. It's a peculiar thing to be out there, when all you can see is that small stretch of ice like a boundless smooth plane of white. Flat, perfectly flat. Nothing changing, nothing moving. It's as though you are sliding along in a field of nothingness. And the only thing that's keeping you sane is the trot of the dogs and their incessant panting.

When you're running a sled, it's essential to get enough calories in you. It's grueling work. And you never sleep enough. So by that sixth day, I was pretty well malnourished and fatigued. My mind was weary from the endless sledding, and it was then during that long stretch that it happened.

I was having a hard time keeping myself awake through the sameness of it all. I caught myself dipping my head on occasion, which is a dangerous thing out there. If you fall off the sled, the dogs will just keep going. And good luck catching up. So I was doing all that I could to keep awake, when suddenly I had this intense feeling as though someone was watching me. Out there in the middle of this nothingness. I lifted up on my toes to look around, and sure enough there was something out there on the ice. A shape that was hard to make out at first through the dull gray mist. But soon I got a better look as my sled got closer, and I knew then that it was a man. He was all dressed up in this fancy white clothing. And as I stared at this man, his features became very clear to me. Those peculiar white clothes were a vestment of sorts, like what the priests wear in a church. A western wind had picked up and was blowing with a hard slant across the ice. The strange thing was that even in that heavy wind, his clothes stayed in place, shining like it was a bright summer day.

The man out on the ice was returning my gaze. It's something that chills me to this day whenever I think about it. That gaze bore down cold into my soul, and I don't think it has ever fully left. It was the first time I'd ever laid eyes on someone that I was sure was wholly evil.

Standing out there alone, I couldn't turn away from him. I felt my fingers slipping from the handlebar, and there seemed to be nothing I could do about it. I was half-convinced I had fallen asleep. The priest's mouth opened wide as if to yell, but what reached my ears was the sound of fracturing ice. It grew louder and louder, until a sudden drop on the right side of the sled sent me reeling. The runner broke through the ice and with it went my foot into the freezing water.

I shifted my weight, but that only served to break the ice even more, and the whole sled began to slowly sink. I was able to crawl over the top and drag myself to safety, holding the leashes to keep my momentum. I tore off my outer boot, which the Inuits called kamik, so as not to let the seawater soak into the first and second layer of footwear. And, of course, the kamik was already frozen solid.

When I looked around, the man in white was nowhere to be found. I called out, but the only answer was the icy blow of the wind across the sheet.

My sled was now in a hopeless situation. It was fairly buoyant, made mostly of ash wood, but the front rails had gone under. Any hope of the dogs pulling it out with leverage were slim. I gave it a shot, but it was no good. It simply floundered and broke more ice as the dogs heaved and jerked against the lead.

I hoped, in a form of miracle, that Alfred or Jørgen would appear and help me drag my sled out of the ice. But with the wind picking up as it was, the Greenlanders were almost assuredly in the process of taking shelter until it passed. And so I was forced to cut the leashes. Ace and the other dogs had been sitting there idly. They watched me with their ice-blue eyes, panting with their illusory smiles as though everything was fine, as I watched my sled, with all my provisions and equipment, disappear slowly into the black waters.

Exhaustion and cold was now taking over. My foot was already going numb. I understood the very real danger of being out on the ice much longer. So I took the dogs inland to find shelter. I left a few markings on the ice. A lash of rope, a loose strap of leather, a pencil jabbed into the ice. I hoped these would mark my position. I also found, along with some pemmican, two matches in my pocket. I kept these. Not very reassuring, but I was still confident that the other dogs, when Alfred passed or Jørgen backtracked, would sniff us out and everything would be alright.

The walk up to shore was not very far, yet in my condition it was an agonizing struggle. The howling wind, coming in from the vast ocean currents, cut through my clothing and bit into my flesh. I shivered as that same uneasy feeling of being watched passed over me. Even worse, I had the sense that I was being followed.

When I was a kid, sleeping in my bed at night, I was certain there was always something lurking behind me, while I lay there in the dark. It was as if my inattention to the shadows would conjure an apparition that would slowly glide across my bedroom, reaching for me. Shivering, I would remain facing the wall. I would never turn around. If I faced the wall all night long, if I did not acknowledge it, then that horrible manifestation would leave me by the morning.

As I walked slowly towards the coast, I had that same feeling of a malignant presence. I never turned around, even when I was sure that whatever was lurking there in the deep cold night was near, and that it was eager for my arrival.

The dogs led the way, as if they sensed what needed to be done, and I followed along blindly. But as we made our way onto the shoreline, where smooth boulders broke through the thin layer of foot ice, the packs' confidence seemed to waiver. Their steps became less sure, their backs bristled as they emitted low growls, staring into the swirling white mist.

A polar bear was my initial thought, but I didn't think a bear would be out in this weather. I shouted commands to the dogs to get them to move forward. They did, reluctantly, still emitting their low, hostile growls.

It had become strangely silent. The wind ceased altogether. My senses strained in that silence as the mist slowly cleared. As I peered forward, a monstrous shape began to form out of that deadening white. A building. The ruins of one that is. It is difficult to explain, but to see that structure, those stacked stones, to see signs of human habitation, out in such an endless white void, you might think was a sublime sight, but I assure you, it was not. It felt more horrifying than seeing one of the great white bears. You must understand, I hadn't seen any permanent structure during the whole expedition, and now, out there in that vast emptiness, I stumbled on something that echoed back to the solid familiar feelings of civilization. It felt unreal, and I half-suspected I had already frozen to death, and this was the entrance to some Arctic underworld.

The roof had collapsed and rotted away long ago, but the walls stood, made of ancient cut stone. A gap in the wall, formed into a cross, overlooked the frozen fjord. It was a church. I thought again of Charles the Fourth and his expeditions to find the lost Norse civilizations of my forefathers. It seemed I had stumbled upon what remained of the church used by those settlers who had vanished so long ago.

The dogs did not want to go inside the church. They hunkered there, hackles raised, growling. And truth be told, I didn't want to go in either. The wind had picked up again. It drifted through the ruins with suggestive whispers that played tricks in my exhausted mind. The roofless church was bathed in moonlight, and it felt as though somehow it was eager for my arrival. It felt alive in its own way. The whole interior of the structure seemed to ooze a menacing presence. My instincts screamed at me to leave, to take my chances out on the ice sheet. But I was too cold, too exhausted. Feeling as though I had no choice, I entered the ruins of the church.

In the northwest corner, there seemed to be a collapsed stairwell of sorts that led underground. The stones near this stairwell were barren of snow. When I finally forced the dogs into the church, they would not go near the stairwell. They bunched in the opposite corner, and I crawled in with them, huddled next to Ace for warmth. He pushed his head against me, and I stroked his ice-riddled fur and gazed up into the sky.

Have you ever seen the northern lights? The stream of the aurorae, how to describe it? It is a river of phantoms, like the slow crossing of the Styx. Souls sliding along on a universal pilgrimage. Bottlegreen, it glows and snakes above your head in a vibrant garden of stars. If I close my eyes, I can still see it. You feel small under it. Very small. I fell asleep within that roofless church, with the dog's hot breath on me and the northern lights dancing amongst the black and the stars.

I dreamt of the church. In the dream it wasn't ruins. It had a beautiful wooden roof, and the cross stood high, pointing towards the long and winding fjord. There were two large ships there in the water, docked. The bright summer sun beat along the rocky shoreline. There was a crowd gathered. The people standing around were starving, emaciated, their eyes filled with desperation and fear. Their clothes ragged, sores covered their sunbeaten faces. Near them, nine timber beams, gleaming in the sun, were spiked along the water's edge. The crowd was looking up at the top of the beams.

On each beam a man hung by his wrists, his neck lashed tight around the beam itself. All of them strangled, like Odin. Nine men for the nine nights Odin hung from the World Tree. This was a desperate measure, a breaking away from Christianity to appease the old gods, to end the famine and save the settlement. All nine faces were bloated and black, their tongues lolled out. There was sorrow in their eyes as the dead men stared down at me.

I felt a presence behind me. I turned, panic seizing my chest. The priest, the one I had seen on the ice, stood in his white robes, holding a long piece of leather. I tried to scream, but only a guttural moan answered. I awoke, shivering, and covered in sweat.

The dogs were gone.

I listened for them, but I met only that overpowering silence. Bone chilling cold, that you'll only find in the Arctic, possessed my body. It felt as if there was just one force in the world, and that was the cold, only the cold, and the cold sought to encase everything in its tomb of ice, to turn the whole world solid and crystalline. My foot was already entombed in its chilling embrace, and I was too cowardly to look and see what I already knew.

But I would not give up so easily. And so I crawled across the floor of the church, across the tumbled stone and frozen soil, to where no dog would tread, to where no frost lay, and where the dark hole in the church floor bloomed. I felt a warmth flowing from there, and with it a fetid breeze, rancid and awful. Yet there was warmth. And warmth is what I desired above all else. So I crawled through the passage of stone without another thought.

I reached within my pocket and pulled out one of my two matches and lit it as I made my way further down into the darkness. It was a cellar of sorts, sloping deeper and deeper underground. When I got to the end of that small underground room, I understood it was not a cellar. It was a crypt.

An alcove was carved out of the earth. Lying in that shadowed pocket was bleached bones and a skull, and the tattered, ancient remains of a priest's garment. And this ghastly tomb, the deepest point within that frozen earth, is where it was warmest. I crawled up to the burial vault like a drowning man to a buoy, my strength fading with each movement forward. If only I could warm up, just a little bit, I felt I could think, I could figure out something, anything to get out of my troubles. The smell was worse, almost unbearable as I crawled closer. The match burned the flesh of my fingers. I didn't care. I curled up, shivering, delirious, at the feet of the priest.

I thought of my mother then, of a time up in the Odense River, where she would take me on summer days and teach me to fish, and I thought of those fish and how beautiful they were in the stream with the water flowing over them, and how that river makes its way out to the ocean, and how the clouds bring it up, up, up again, back over land. There is a beautiful cycle to nature, and I was part of it.

I drifted into unconsciousness with those strange thoughts floating in my mind, and I dreamt I was at the top of an immensely tall pole that went high up into the sky. My hands were tied to the top of the pole. I could see all of Denmark below me. I could see my home. I could see the brook where I caught fish as a boy. I could see all those that I loved.

But I knew something was climbing the pole, climbing towards me. When I looked down, I saw the priest. I saw his hateful eyes as he crawled, like a spider crawls. I looked away, trying to take in as much of the world as I could, to take in all the mountains and the streams and the lakes and the trees and how the clouds moved as they did. I could feel the priest's breath on me, as he whispered from behind, 'Isn't It beautiful?' I felt his cold hands on my neck, tightening. I began to scream, but again nothing would come out.

When I awoke, it was pitch black. I knew the priest was there with me in the crypt. I fumbled desperately for my last match, praying it would strike. It didn't at first, the damn thing, but soon it took, and the shadows retreated quickly, and with them the priest. I crawled out of that basement, out into the open air, out onto the frozen shoreline, along the white bleak tundra. I could hear the priest's laughter. Fear and desperation pushed me on. If I was to die, at least I would die away from that god-forsaken church.

And then I couldn't crawl anymore. I had nothing left to give. I collapsed on the cold ice, which didn't feel so cold anymore. I looked back, and I saw the priest then, making his way slowly, confidently, through the mist with his hungry smile. I gazed up into the sky, where the northern lights danced. I felt that same feeling of nature's cycle. I heard the priest whisper in my ear, "isn't it beautiful?"

I accepted then that I was going to die, and that I was okay with it.

Then the priest was shaking me, shouting my name. But it wasn't the priest. No, it was Alfred. Old normal, body-and-soul Alfred standing there above me. I could hear the dogs barking. And that was that. They had found me. Ace had located the other pack and brought them.

Alfred loaded me up in the sled and we returned to camp.

I lost my foot. The doctor took it off there in the camp right soon as we got back. I spent the next few months in and out of a fever. But by the coming of spring, I was healthy enough to head back to Copenhagen, where I have been ever since.

And that's my story, that's when I saw a ghost. Or I saw something, at least, and it wasn't alive.

WALK ON
Alan Hardy

Fallen boughs assume creepy shapes,
of bodiless limbs of crouching humans,
half-limbed reptiles hugging the earth.
Lying still in undergrowth, in wait. Camouflaged.
You open the door at night and walk into darkness,
imagine shadows and terrors, and hidden monsters.
It's the time it takes to fumble a lock or chain and scamper back inside.
Sometimes, though, you look up and see a face
consumed by hatred, a burst of madness, someone you love.
It lasts longer. Your body quakes. You feel pain. You must face
the shock. You survive. The days pass. You return to what you were.
Someone who, wandering along the path,
meets the gaze of a bewitched piece of wood,
a slap from the primeval past, its imaginings.
Then you walk on. And on. Until, one day, the real terror comes.

The Astrakhan Coat
Piertommaso Spagnuolo

Ivan lived in one of those ancient seaside towns, so old it seemed oblivious to the very history of its existence, reeking of the sea at every moment of the day—a place teeming with countless faces, each marked by a singular trait, sculpted by the salt-laden air itself.

His family, one of those whose name had echoed through the annals and registries of the town for as long as memory could stretch, was as rich in tales and legends as it was poor in wealth—especially since his grandfather, once a fabulously wealthy and eccentric shipowner, had lost everything and mysteriously vanished.

Some claimed he had squandered his immense fortune at the gaming tables, while others said he was surrounded by a horde of equally eccentric lovers, whose numbers grew too vast to be sustained by his dwindling finances.

Another legend, more macabre and less credible even by the eccentric standards of that family and the peculiar little town itself, whispered of a life devoted to something far darker—something unspeakable—that in the end consumed him utterly.

At some point, he had simply disappeared into nothingness, leaving behind a wife, children, entire attics filled with ancient knick-knacks, and a mystery that *no one dared to investigate fully*.

While Ivan's uncles had paid off their share of debts through hard labour and spent their youth studying law or medicine to secure their futures, his father had not been granted the same opportunity. Instead, he devoted his life to writing—in a time and place where the written word was almost forgotten. His modest teaching job at the local high school, together with his mother's work as a seamstress, was never enough to bring financial stability.

Ivan, for his part, was still too young to concern himself with such matters, yet the economic crisis faced by his parents still touched him in other ways. From the time he was a child, he had delighted in immersing himself in the depths of the cellar or the attics of his family villa, digging through old trunks in search of treasures that his ancestors—especially his grandfather, a great traveller and explorer—might have hidden.

Each time he stumbled upon an unsettling African mask, a curious and ancient cross-shaped ring, or a votive statuette of some forgotten pagan deity, the result was always the same. "Does it have any value?" his father would ask, a man who, over time, had lost any semblance of passion for historical or even mysterious artifacts, developing instead a full-blown obsession with finances. "If it has value, sell it; if not, throw it away." That was the rule.

Ivan, who loved his parents and, in certain ways, sensed the financial suffering they endured, complied without a word, never keeping anything for himself. He came into possession of a mysterious artifact, and by the following week, all he could do was watch it from the display case of a downtown antique shop.

On a gloomy November afternoon, one like all the others, heavy with rain and that cold, maritime humidity that seeps into your bones, Ivan was rummaging through the mysteries of one of the many storerooms in his attic, searching for yet another fragment of history that his father would force him to sell. It was at that moment, after shifting a stack of old, discarded chairs, that he found himself facing a wooden wardrobe he had never seen before. It had a timeless, weighty presence, and it seemed as though no one had opened it in many years.

Its doors were adorned with decorative inlays he couldn't quite place, yet they vaguely resembled Eastern art. Not Arabic, nor Asian, and certainly not European, but rather the kind of enigmatic artistry that hails from places where all these cultures merge.

In its lock, as Ivan noted with great astonishment and excitement, was a key made of solid gold, which alone would likely equal a month's wages of both his parents combined. The decorations on the handle were perfectly identical to those on the wardrobe itself, a detail that made him realize the strange piece of furniture hailed from the same time and place.

With the excitement that only a boy of his age could feel in the face of mystery, Ivan reached out and turned the key in the lock, slowly opening the creaking doors of the wardrobe and letting himself be engulfed by a stifling waft of old, musty scent.

Almost intimidated by the ancient smell, the boy thought of retreating. A shiver ran down his spine, and for an instant, he almost felt as if he were touching secrets he should never have touched. Despite this, driven by his immense childlike curiosity, he retrieved his trusty flashlight and stretched out into the vast wardrobe, which, if possible, was even larger and more spacious than it had appeared from the outside.

Inside, he did not find the immense treasures that his mind had painted the moment he had glimpsed those Eastern decorations, but instead a simple, mouldy—though majestic—black astrakhan coat.

Despite his mother's profession, Ivan was not particularly interested in fashion. He wore whatever she sewed for him, but to him, clothes were only what they were meant to be: they kept the dampness of that cursed seaside town from his bones and helped him adhere to the rules of good manners. That coat, however, had something strange about it. It struck him immediately, captivating him more than any other unsettling artifact he had ever found in the depths of his old, dilapidated villa. It almost seemed to emanate an *aura*—both mysterious and unsettling.

Without thinking twice, in a gesture completely natural for a boy his age, he took the coat from its hanger and held it in his arms, noticing how soft and heavy it was. He traced the fabric's stripes with his cold-numbed fingers, feeling a strange pull emanating from it. Almost as if the coat itself wanted to be worn. And so, he did, though with an inexplicable sense of unease creeping over him.

Slowly, he took it by the collar and lifted it in front of him, slipping one sleeve on, then the other, letting the shoulders fall across his body, wrapping him like an old but luxurious blanket. Immediately, he felt a sense of relief, almost as if the coat had the power to warm him in a way that no other garment his mother had ever sewn could.

Ivan turned toward one of the many dusty mirrors scattered about the attic, his gaze falling upon the coat draped over his frame. Its length was almost absurd, the hem brushing against his ankles—a garment clearly fashioned for a figure far taller than any man born of earthly proportions. And yet, it possessed an undeniable majesty, a grandeur so intoxicating that he could not help but imagine himself cloaked in the imperious authority of a bygone monarch. It exuded a sense of ancient opulence, as though it had once graced the shoulders of a king whose name had been whispered through the corridors of time.

It was then that he slipped his hands into the pockets, absentmindedly, and his fingers sensed a myriad of secrets buried within.

With the calm of an archaeologist unearthing a relic from the bare earth, the boy grasped a small, cold metal container, turning it over in his hands, partially concealed by the sleeves of his coat.

It was a silver tobacco case, decorated with patterns he was certain he'd seen before.

Items like this were displayed on an old, lacquered table at his uncles' house, while at his own home, they were buried in a drawer along with his mother's buttons and threads. Ivan immediately understood that this object, like the coat, could only have belonged to his grandfather—a man he had never met, having vanished many years before his birth, yet one he felt he knew through the old daguerreotypes. In them, his grandfather – a man small in stature but fierce in gaze - was depicted with his faithful ivory pipe, a cryptic smile, and pale, shadowed eyes that seemed both ominous and otherworldly.

He opened it, his breath catching with the faint hope of uncovering some small, long-forgotten treasure.

Instead, what greeted him was a crumbling mass of withered tobacco, its acrid scent steeped in the decay of countless decades. But far worse was the nest of grotesque sea insects that stirred within. They were small, yet unnervingly swift, their segmented bodies glistening like damp, blackened shells. Their legs, too many to count, moved with a horrible precision, and their bulbous eyes glimmered with an unnatural, alien hunger. As if offended by the intrusion, they surged forth in a frenzied tide, their chittering filling the silence of the attic. They began to crawl up the tarnished silver walls of the box, their trajectory unwavering as they reached toward the boy's trembling hands, their movements deliberate, almost intelligent.

Ivan, in a frightened and instinctive gesture, dropped it to the ground, kicking it away with the toe of his boot and a horrified, stifled cry.

For a moment, the boy was overtaken by a shiver of disgust at the thought that the old coat—so magnificent and regal—might harbour a colony of horrific insects. He almost considered taking it off and tossing it back into the wardrobe, closing it behind him and trapping those little demonic creatures once again in the hell of dust and mold from which they had come.

Despite this, he slipped his hand back into the pocket, and it was then that his fingers grasped a piece of paper. Ivan unfolded it before his eyes, squinting to see better in the dim November light.

It was then that, puzzled, he read a simple message, written in faded black ink on paper that looked older than the villa itself.

"Hello, Ivan."

The boy shuddered, his eyes widening, blinking rapidly as he tried to make sense of what he was seeing. Was he dreaming? Was this message some kind of trick his mind was playing on him?

In a gesture of disdain, firmly convinced that it could only be a hallucination, he crumpled the paper and tossed it aside, slipping his hands back into the pockets. He pulled out another piece of paper, one he could have sworn he hadn't noticed before.

"Don't you want to talk to me?" he read, the words seeming to echo in his mind, unsettling and almost too direct, as though the paper itself were aware of his every thought.

"What..." Ivan exclaimed, surprised and, in some ways, disturbed by the strange situation. "... Who are you?" he whispered, his voice barely audible in the afternoon silence of the attic, as he slipped his hands back into the pockets, expecting to find yet another note.

"I think you've already figured that out." Came the response from the mysterious source buried deep within the soft depths of the pockets.

"Grandpa?" Ivan whispered again, glancing around with the cautious manner of someone who expected to be caught at any moment in the middle of some unknown sorcery.

The response was slow to come, strangely slow, and the boy rummaged further into the pockets, fearing for a moment that the mysterious conversation had abruptly ended without any explanation.

But, after a few seconds, he found yet another note.

"Exactly," it finally read.

The hours and days that followed seemed to slip away, entirely consumed by that ceaseless and bizarre dialogue —a strange, unrelenting bridge that spanned the yawning chasm between his bleak, monotonous reality and some grotesque, otherworldly dimension, one that seemed as ancient as time itself. It was as though this unseen realm had claimed his grandfather long ago, pulling him into its dark, unfathomable depths, where he had been devoured by forces beyond human comprehension. Each passing moment felt like a step deeper into that same abyss, as if the very fabric of his existence were beginning to unravel, thread by thread, under the weight of secrets too terrible to be borne.

Of course, he was wise enough not to speak of it to his parents, who nonetheless noticed his strange evasiveness and the morbid way he secluded himself in the attic—odd, even for a treasure hunter like him. But on the other hand, they were both far too engrossed in their own pursuits to concern themselves with a boy who, otherwise meek, had more than sufficiently demonstrated that he required no special attention.

Through those brittle, yellowed scraps of paper, his grandfather recounted his seafaring adventures with an intensity that almost seemed to transcend the limitations of mortal memory. The words, though faint and worn by the passage of countless years, seemed to pulse with a life of their own, as though the very ink had been steeped in the salty air of forgotten oceans. He spoke of ancient treasures, their allure unmatched by anything the world had since known—golden relics from civilizations long devoured by the abyss, whose very names had been erased from history. Of mermaids, too, he spoke, not the whimsical, seductive creatures of popular lore, but beings of dark and unknowable origin, whose eyes glimmered with secrets too terrible for any man to grasp. And there were tales of mysterious ruins, hidden beneath the vast and restless sea, where the ocean itself seemed to guard ancient horrors best left undisturbed—ruins so old that even time itself appeared to tremble in their presence, as if the earth itself feared the dark knowledge buried beneath the crushing weight of the waves.

But Ivan never had the courage to ask that simple yet unsettling question that slithered in his mind. At least not until, captivated by yet another timeless story, he finally decided to confront the strange matter head-on.

"Grandpa, can I ask you something?" Ivan whispered, in another bleak afternoon near December. "Of course." Came the swift and faithful reply, as always, from the other side of that absurd conversation. "Where are you?" Ivan whispered, almost frightened. "I mean... right now."

"*I thought you would never ask*" the ink on the paper responded, now in a more cursive script, almost impatiently, as though his grandfather were reproaching him for not having already asked such an obvious question.

Ivan did not respond immediately, almost intimidated by the authoritative nature of the answer and the question he had just asked. He reached into his pockets once more, and for the first time since finding the astrakhan coat, he retrieved a piece of paper with an answer to a question he hadn't even asked yet.
"Do you want to see it?"

That very afternoon, as the feeble light filtering through the dense, oppressive clouds shrouding the seaside town gave way to the eerie yet strangely familiar dusk, Ivan laboriously stuffed the coat into an old, weathered backpack. Grasping one of his creaking, ancient fishing rods, he pieced together a feeble charade for his parents. With a quick step and a murmured, half-convincing excuse, he slipped out the door.

"I'm off to fish by the rocks," he muttered to his father, who sat hunched at the kitchen table, immersed in the grim arithmetic of balancing their meagre accounts, and to his mother, who sewed by the fireplace where, just hours before, they had cast the remnants of a mouldering wooden board into the flames—enough to warm them briefly without the ruinous expense of proper firewood.

As soon as he was far enough from the villa, walking along the jagged coastline that separated it from the sea, he retrieved the coat from his backpack and slipped it on. He followed the line of the rocks, heading toward the precise spot where his grandfather had suggested they meet.

The few fishermen lingering nearby, already packing up their gear to return home at this late hour, cast curious glances at the peculiar sight: a somewhat awkward boy, wrapped in a coat of astrakhan far too grand and oversized for his frame, making his way across the foam-slick cliffs. The regal and gigantic garment, incongruous against the salt-crusted desolation of the shore, seemed almost to grant him an air of spectral otherworldliness.

"And now?" Ivan whispered, his feet struggling to maintain balance on the jagged tips of the rocks as the tide slowly rose, reflecting the darkness of the sky. "Look into my eyes in the sea," replied the ink on paper once more.

It was then that Ivan leaned slightly forward, fixing his gaze on the dark waters churning below, unaware of the marine insects beginning to emerge from the rocks like an ominous prelude.

Not for a moment did the boy consider that perhaps his mysterious correspondent might not be his grandfather, but something else entirely. At least, not until he began to discern, in the depths of the water, a terrifying source of green gloom shaped like an eye, so intense that it pierced through the waves and illuminated even the folds of that old, musty coat. An abhorrent underwater sun, shining with an unreal green glow, the likes of which he had never seen and could never hope to see.

"Do you see me?" asked a voice this time, deep and unsettling, seeming to bubble up from within the rising tide, while the crown of that greenish sun pulsated, branching ever further with glowing, unnatural corals.

Then, in an instant, the waves grew fiercer, washing the sea insects off the rocks and soaking the boy's legs and boots, almost like hands reaching from the water to grasp at them.

Ivan, frightened and disoriented, had no time to flee from the rocks, too sharp to climb easily—especially for someone weighed down by such a heavy coat, which seemed to grow heavier and heavier, hindering his every move. The water was greenish, luminous as well, as if it carried with it something malevolent, infused by that radiant source.

A sudden, monstrous rogue wave, borne from the chaotic heart of the sea, crashed over him with an unnatural ferocity, dragging him mercilessly into the cold, inky depths, toward an unknown place—an unfathomable underwater realm or hidden dimension. Perhaps the very one where his grandfather had vanished a century ago-.

Leaving behind... yet another mystery *no one dared to investigate fully*.

Skull Crow by Warren Muzak

Watching
D J Tyrer

Most peculiar thing...
Eyes in the wall watching me
Not all the time... no
Not always there... but often
Eyes malevolent and strange
Not looking through peepholes
But manifest in some way I cannot explain
Dead and staring
Meaning unknown
Their obsession with me a mystery
Did I somehow do them wrong?
Or, do they hunger for a sight of life
Denied to them now?
I do not know...
All they do is watch...

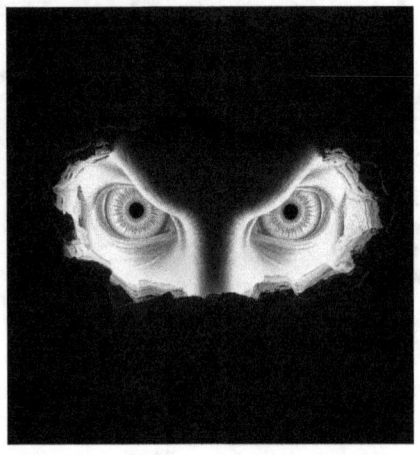

The Window-Room
Jen Mierisch

Some of us are dead, you see, long before we were ready to be. I'd borne seven children and lost one already, and I'd sooner be damned than watch them take my Rose. Can you blame me for doing what I did, to save my baby from an early grave? Do you blame me? Is that why I linger, here in the dark?

***

At sea, April 1888

Blood is my earliest memory. My mother, on her knees, in the corner near the sinks, on the dim steerage deck during our voyage. The dirty sheets someone had placed beneath her, soaked with spreading crimson. Her face, screwed up in pain as cramps gripped her body like the powerful waves outside. Her eyes, opening once, finding my half-brother. "Francesco," she gasped, "take Lina away," as if there were anywhere to go in that space, crammed with Italians like us who had sold everything to get to Napoli and buy our steamship tickets. I suppose Mama thought she would spare me. I suppose she thought a four-year-old girl could have some time, yet, to be innocent of these matters. But I was soon to know them, as women do, whether we are ready or not.

The only doctor on board was in first class. As he descended the stairs, his nose wrinkled at the smell of us, unwashed as we hundreds were, with no bathing facilities in steerage. I felt surprised to see him make such a face; none of us noticed the odor any more after seven days at sea. Still, it was good to see him and his leather bag with its shiny clasps. Doctors were fine people who healed the sick. He would help Mama.

The doctor was tall and had a brown moustache. He swung into action, opening his bag, bending over my mother to listen to her heart through a long tube. Then he stood, looked around, and located my father, who sat on the floor with his knees drawn up, looking as if he were ill himself.

"Are you her husband?"

"Yes. Husband." Papa knew about twenty words in English. He'd memorized "husband," "wife," "son," and "daughter" to speak to the immigration officials after our arrival in New York.

"What is her name?"

"Rosa. Rosa Girolanda."

"Is she with child?"

Papa blinked, uncomprehending. He turned to us. "Francesco," he said in Italian, "find out what the man wants."

My brother, who had picked up quite a bit of English from hanging around the docks after school, stepped forward boldly. "She is with two children," he announced with pride. "Me, I am Francesco. My sister, Michelina."

"Erm," said the doctor with a funny smile. "I mean to say..." He put a hand over his stomach and looked at me. I understood right away.

"She is in the family way," I said. "We're going to have a little brother or sister in America." *Preferably a sister*, I did not add. I don't remember which language I spoke. I don't remember not knowing English. Francesco might have translated. Papa moaned and lowered his head between his knees.

The doctor nodded and bent over my mother once more. A woman with gray hair tied into a bun knelt next to Mama, took her hand, and whispered. I don't know if she prayed, offered comfort, or translated the doctor's directions. After the boat docked, I never saw her again.

Mama's face was pale, her brow moist with sweat. Blood had trimmed the hems of her skirts. She closed her eyes again, hard enough to force tears down her cheeks, and clenched her jaw as if making a great effort not to cry out. After a while, she had to lay back, and the passengers who had been watching turned their heads away. As the doctor worked, my mother murmured prayers to God and Santa Catherina.

I saw it when they took it away. The gray-haired woman tried to bundle up the blood-soaked sheets, but I saw. It had a head, and a body, but its arms and legs were shriveled, like a tomato left too long on the windowsill. Its belly looked fat, just like it ought, like it should have been robust enough. Its eyes were shut, like a newborn farm cat's, blind to the flood of fluid and pain in which it had been born and died. It was small enough to fit in the palm of my mother's hand, if she had held it.

Nobody would tell me where they took him. I dreamed he became a fish, swimming alongside our boat. I don't know why I thought he was a boy, but I felt as certain as anything.

He was too tiny to live, and too young to baptize. And my mother's prayers went unanswered. And just like that, I learned God was someone who could not be counted upon.

I didn't have a sister until three years later.

***

It's dark here in this in-between place. It is as dim as the steerage decks, yet beautiful in its way, lit by the glow from the windows.

Each of us has a window through which we can see the world on the other side, the people we've left behind. We can see and hear them, but we cannot touch, cannot pass through. Naturally, we spend most of our time watching at our windows, looking in on our families and friends.

Some of us are dead, you see, too soon, when we were right in the middle of things. Rafaelle Cuozzo retired one month before Death stole him away from his favorite chair where he tickled giggling grandchildren on his lap. Vincenza Branca was planning her wedding when the consumption took her; she wept for her lost future and to see her fiancé despondent at her bedside. And Serafina Lupo was but eleven when she arrived, the first blush of beauty on her olive skin, her head still bloody from the horse's kick. I wrapped my arms around the small, frightened girl and helped her find her window. She was the same age my Tonia would have been, if scarlet fever hadn't claimed her, but that is too painful to speak of.

Catholics, Protestants, and many others, we all come here, and after a time, we leave. I cannot predict when it is someone's time to leave; it is a secret whispered by an unseen speaker. When Rafaelle Cuozzo turned away from his window, his wrinkled face gazed into the darkness at the edge of our space, yet his face lit up with a peace, a contentment, that I envied, before he walked slowly forth and vanished. They all look like that when they go. But some don't go quickly. Some remain here for some time, as I know well.

I do not know where I am, but for want of a name, I call it the window-room.

***

New York, 1890s-1900s

I loved our life in Brooklyn. Even as a child, I left home as often as Mama let me, volunteering for every errand, delivering every message to our cousins up the road. Our first tenement dwelling was a cold-water apartment, stifling in summer and drawing us shivering to the coal stove in winter. Leaving it was both a joy and a relief.

Never had I dreamed there could be so many kinds of people. Old and young, penniless and wealthy, shouting to one another in German, Scotch, Russian, Polish. A few spoke Yiddish, using their hands almost as much as my family did, and what storytellers they were! Some New Yorkers had skin as brown as tree bark, and others had hair as yellow as fresh-made pasta. My favorite chores took me to Flatbush Avenue, where I could watch the streetcars rumble by, hear the clomp of horses' hooves as they pulled carriages, and smell hot food cooking, from potato knishes to fresh-baked rye.

At first, Mama wouldn't let me go out without Francesco. But one day, he beat two Irish boys' faces bloody, even though they'd ambushed us in an alley (I got in a few scratches for good measure). After that, the older kids left both of us alone.

The city was colorful, chaotic, and full of wonders. This was exactly how I wanted to live: to ride the current of this fast-moving river, to thrive in its vibrant energy, to never, ever stop moving. School and church and home life were as predictable as the sun, but on the streets of

Brooklyn, every day one saw something fascinating, or horrifying, but always new.

"Don't grow up too fast, Lina," Mama said with a smile, but she was glad to have me out and about to fetch and carry, with Papa working and three younger ones to look after.

I expect in many ways I was a disappointment as an eldest daughter. Fortunately, my sister Violetta was my opposite. Where I lacked the patience to be still, she could sit for hours, mending or reading. When she wasn't helping Mama fry zucchini flowers or bathe our little brothers, Letta was at the library searching out stories. She told me those stories late at night, in the bed we shared, and my mind would drift off to arctic ice-floes and ghostly moors until it quieted.

When I first saw Antonio, I was fifteen, walking home from the market on a sun-soaked July morning. A delivery wagon stood parked at the curb. Antonio perched in the driver's seat, one hand holding the reins and the other lifting a cigarette to his lips. He was blond, blue-eyed, and striking; I thought he must be Norwegian. What a surprise when his colleague hopped up next to him and they spoke in fluent Italian. I was in the new dress I'd made, the one that cousin Ella said "gave me a figure." I walked past with a bounce so my skirts would swish. His eyes lingered on me before he flicked the cigarette into the gutter and slapped the reins to move the horses. The next day, his eyes lingered longer.

Antonio was smart, irreverent, and fascinated with new ideas. When we strolled together in Prospect Park, he carried on about the latest inventions (electric light-bulbs!) and showed me magazines with pictures of the can-can dancers at the Moulin Rouge. He had a quick wit that matched my own. I adored him body and soul.

We married at the court-house on an autumn Thursday when the leaves turned the streets red and gold. I told the clerk I was eighteen, because I was days away from turning sixteen, and sixteen was close enough. My parents would have liked me to wait, but a pale-haired northern Italian was still Italian, and at least he was

Catholic.

Our sons James and John arrived one after the other, and I became wholly consumed with looking after them and loving them. With the arrival of our daughter Mariantonia, who we called Tonia, Antonio's parents' flat was becoming too crowded for all of us. My husband found us a house across town, small but perfect. His delivery business had progressed from horses to motor-trucks, and he had charge of twenty novice drivers.

We were all of us delighted with the house, but that first Sunday, when we dressed in our best and walked to the Catholic church across the street, we were in for a shock. The blue-eyed deacon stood out front and shook his head. "No Italians, I'm afraid," he said with kind of smile that's sweet on the outside and sour beneath. "What a time! So many immigrants, blessed with so many children of God. Our pews are filled!" He turned to the red-haired family just approaching. "Ah, Mr. and Mrs. Quinn! A pleasure to see you this morning."

Antonio's face darkened. He turned on his heel and marched us down the block to the Methodist church. And just like that, we were Protestants. It was all the same to me. The name didn't matter; it was but different ways to worship the same God, if He noticed us at all.

And yet, names did matter. Surrounded by new congregants (and potential clients) from all over Europe, my husband began introducing himself as Tony. When the census taker came around, on a whim, I gave my own first name as Maggie. This was now our country, after all, and we needed to fit in.

Our parents were not pleased with these developments, but my beloved sister Violetta was my steadfast friend. She had married at eighteen and had two daughters, whom she often brought across town on the street-car to visit. They adored my daughter Tonia and played happily on the stoop together.

Soon we had two more sons, Ray and Tommy, and our small house seemed ever smaller. My wish had been granted: I never stopped moving. Yet at times I wondered how many more blessings I could manage.

***

Here in the window-room, our lingering and longing is mixed with joy. Though they mourn, our loved ones move on, with families to feed and money to earn, and we watch the children play.

Sometimes, in the gloaming hours when the world's dimness matches that of our own, someone looks through the window from the other side. They sit up in bed, or stop in their tracks, and stare, wide-eyed, at one of us. Very seldom indeed, they speak with their loved one through the glass. We all gather around to witness such rare events, at a modest distance out of respect, hoping we might have our turn.

It's a lovely place, for what it is. The windows are not in sashes or frames; rather, their borders are as rough and random as those of a country pond. The glass gleams, though I expect it is not true glass, but something more mysterious. If you touch it, its surface shimmers and moves, like quicksilver spilled from a broken thermometer. Please believe me: I truly did not mean to spoil such a splendid thing.

The first thing I saw through my window was my own pale face, eyes closed, my lifeless body laid out in my bed, the familiar crack in the wall snaking toward the ceiling. Nestled next to me, three-year-old Marie slept, her blond curls sticking out as wildly as ever, her chubby cheeks streaked with dried-up streams of tears. In her slumber, she pulled her thumb from her mouth and wrapped her tiny arm around my waist.

My turn for the miracle came sooner than I'd imagined. The day after my arrival, I peered through my window at my sister Violetta. Moonlight painted her face as she lay in bed, where her husband Giovanni snored lightly at her side. Her wide-awake eyes were toward the sky, where a near-full moon blazed among brilliant stars. Her head turned, and her eyes met mine. She gasped in surprise but showed no trace of fear. I smiled to see her, and she smiled back at me.

"My dear sister," I said. "I love you."

"Lina," she whispered. "Are you really here?"

"I miss you, Letta," was all I could reply.

Her eyes welled up then. "I miss you, too," she said. "I wish you didn't have to go."

The window glass began to mist over, as it sometimes does, shifting like sunset shadows.

"Please," I said, "watch over my babies." Violetta nodded in silent promise.

***

New York, 1910s

By 1914, we had five children, given to us by God or fate. When Tonia died, I might have wondered if God punished us for rejecting the church and the names with which we'd been baptized. However, there was little to wonder about. More than half of my daughter's class succumbed to the scarlet fever that year, the good children and the bad, and the school was closed, but I will not speak of that, or I shall not have the strength to finish my tale.

Our second daughter came during the Great War. Though she was the second, she was the eldest still living, and so, as was the custom, we named her for Antonio's mother, just as we had the first. I could not bear to call her by the same name as her lost sister, so we called her Marie. In 1918, we named our third daughter Rose, after my mother.

At first, the Spanish Flu was a faraway thing, a sad malaise afflicting the soldiers in the war trenches. We heard of deaths in the city, especially in the crowded tenements. We read the numbers in the papers, but our community remained mostly untouched ("the hearty Mediterranean diet!" Papa insisted). It is a strange puzzle in our human nature that when one person dies, we are devastated, but one thousand dying means little more than one thousand grains of sand sifting through one's fingers at the Coney Island beach.

When our neighbor, that ancient character Arcangela Borgia, fell ill in January of 1919, I thought nothing of taking food to her and passing the time while baby Rose napped. A cantankerous widow, Arcangela was never one to hold back a saucy opinion, and it was an amusement to listen to her stories about the old country. Besides, with the war over, surely the worst of the epidemic had passed.

After a week or two, Arcangela pulled through and resumed haranguing her grandchildren about how they shouldn't trust the Irish. By February, however, it was clear that the illness had passed to me. When my fever flared, I kept on with the marketing and washing and cooking, having little choice with six children to manage. Soon I felt so weak that rising from bed became impossible. My head throbbed, my throat burned, and my body shook with chills. Violetta, who lived near enough to our parents that Mama could mind her babies, came across town to keep the house and look after her nieces and nephews.

Antonio said the influenza wouldn't take me. Look at your strong constitution, giving birth to seven babies since seventeen, he said, as if I were a prize heifer, as if childbirth had made me invincible instead of tired. The cholera took Lizzy Miller, but not you, he told me. Lillian DeVita died from eclampsia of pregnancy, but it never touched you. He sounded sure, but he sat some distance from me, though I longed for his touch on my hand. He left the room quickly, and traces of fear haunted his eyes.

I worried less about myself than my children. The boys and Marie seemed healthy, but baby Rose coughed the whole night long for five days.

My fever broke, but the sickness had soured and crept deep into my chest. Between crushing bouts of coughing, I was aware of Arcangela entering my room to clear the rags into which I had expelled unnatural-looking fluids. She glanced at my face and drew back in shock. How must I have looked, to provoke such a reaction in an old woman who had seen everything?

My fingers turned black, and then my wrists, and drawing breath became a soggy task, as if my lungs were leaky ships filling slowly with ocean water. Fear seized me then, and I prayed, skeptic or no. I received no reply but a gush of blood, which ran from my nose with the swiftness of a spring thaw. As I gasped and wheezed, my panicked thoughts whirled like a tempest threatening to drown me.

I cannot die. I am but thirty-four. Antonio cannot manage any of this alone. What will become of my babies?

***

Today, through my window, I see my daughters' bedroom. The sky outside is gray, as if a storm nears. Tepid light bathes the room, casting the corners into shadow.

My sister Violetta and my daughter Marie sit together on Marie's small bed. Violetta holds her niece on her lap, tousling her curls, while Marie plays with a rag rabbit. Across the room, my mother stands next to the crib, where baby Rose lies asleep. Mama nudges the cradle-basket so that it rocks in its swinging frame. She lets it go and slowly crosses the room to sit on the bed beside my sister.

The room is terribly quiet. I worry at the silence within the crib, willing Rose to cough. Then the women murmur in Italian, and I strain to hear.

"Your papa sent for him," says Mama. "The Italian undertaker. He should arrive at any moment."

"All right," says Violetta. "I hope he is not hungry. I have not cooked anything today. It is all I can do to manage the house, even with Arcangela's help."

A cough comes from the crib. It is gentler than when I heard it last it. My heart leaps; perhaps Rose's condition has improved.

The women's heads turn, and a man comes into the room holding his hat in his hands. He is short, stout, and curly-haired. He nods at each woman in turn.

"I am sorry for your loss," he says. "Michelina is with God."

I scoff at that. I cannot help myself. "When you arrive," I say, though he will not hear, "you tell me if God is here or not."

Mama is crossing herself. Violetta has cast her eyes downward, but at the same time, cocks her head slightly, as if she has heard me speak.

"I shall take Michelina with me when I leave today," the man continues, "if you would like to say a final goodbye."

The word hits me like a falling tree. A final goodbye? What will happen when my body leaves my house? Will I still have my window to look through? The thought of such a deprivation, after all that I have lost, grips my heart, and I begin to weep.

Mama nods at the man's words. Violetta frowns and looks toward the wall, almost in my direction.

"If you like," says the undertaker, "I will take the baby as well."

Mama looks up. Violetta's head snaps toward the man. "What?"

"The young ones, they do not survive the influenza," says the undertaker with a shake of his head. "I have taken three this week. Look at her, the poor lamb, so quiet."

Violetta looks at Rose, who is still and peaceful, her little chest rising and falling. "But she is not dead."

"Two losses can be difficult to bear," says the man solemnly. "I am sorry. For the baby, it is but a matter of time."

My heart slams against my chest. My mother and sister look at one another.

"I visit Brooklyn only twice per week," says the man, "and if baby shares with mama, you will have but one coffin to purchase."

I cannot watch any longer. I lurch forward. A shriek rips from my gut. "No!" I throw myself against the window. Its surface quivers.

Violetta looks up sharply, but she sees only the wall. Though the room is dim, it is day, and she cannot see me.

"Please, Letta," I cry, "do not let him take my baby."

Letta faces Mama. "Lina would not want us to give her daughter up," she says.

"It is very expensive, Letta," Mama says in a low voice. "Babies are not strong creatures. Sometimes they die."

"Lina's babies are strong," says Letta.

"Tonia was not," murmurs Mama.

Violetta's face is stricken. She hugs Marie on her lap, covers the child's ears, and kisses her curls.

"Your brother Gaetano was not," whispers Mama, who

has closed her eyes. I stare at her, agape. She has never spoken of that day on the boat. I never knew he had a name. Babies born too early did not have names, at least not in the eyes of God.

"Well..." Tears stream silently down my sister's face. She looks at baby Rose.

The undertaker steps forward. He is crossing the room. He is striding toward the crib, reaching out his hands.

"NO!" I leap against the glass. The place where I hit is darkened, scarred. I ram it again. More cracks, splintering its surface.

The dead watch me with their mouths open. A woman wails. They must worry that I am breaking sacrosanct laws, that I will be damned. But I know, with my body and soul, what would be worse than that.

I step back and run at the window with all my power. A deafening *snap* splits the air in the window-room. The pane breaks loose, and for a moment I'm certain I hear the glass screaming.

Then I am through, tumbling onto the floor of my daughters' room. The force of my entry is too violent; I cannot halt my motion. I crash into the crib. Its cradle swings wildly, and I watch in horror as baby Rose tips out onto the rug.

My mother and sister gasp, but they do not see me. They see Rose, who cries fiercely, lustfully, with hale, hearty lungs that are absolutely clear.

Violetta hands Marie off to Mama, jumps forward, and scoops up my baby. Rose's cheeks are round, her fists pink and strong, her temperament as fervent as my own.

The undertaker stands frozen, blinking, shaking his head as if to clear the vision of what he has witnessed, which is not logical. A cradle cannot tip over on its own.

Violetta clutches Rose and turns to the man. With her head held high, she tells him, "The baby will stay with us."

***

Some of us are dead, you see, with our stories unfinished, our endings unwritten. We breathed deeply, we loved ardently, we lived vigorously with every ounce of ourselves, yet our books contain blank pages.

As soon as I heard Violetta dismiss the undertaker, when I saw her holding baby Rose, I felt the window-room pulling back whatever pieces of me had broken through. Fighting that force would have been as futile as swimming against the currents that carry one out to sea.

I had saved my daughter, but I had destroyed my window. It swung shut behind me, its surface marred and darkened, and thus it remained. I, too, have remained, always near. But whatever substance the glass may be, once broken, it is not a thing that heals.

I peer through others' windows when they let me, but the window-room is crowded, and I do not often encounter among the new arrivals someone that I knew in life. A man who had worked with my husband told me that Antonio had remarried, and his new wife was Irish. Antonio had kept all four boys, but the man knew nothing about Marie and Rose.

After three years, Arcangela arrived, and I drank up her news like one dying of thirst in the desert. Violetta had adopted Marie, who had started school and loved to read. Baby Rose had gone to cousin Fortunata, whom I did not know well, but at the time of my death she was the only cousin who had room in the house and was still breastfeeding. Rose, now three and a half, had lovely brown curls, was as active as her mother, and thrived, though she pestered her adopted siblings with her constant singing.

Papa arrived ten years later, and our reunion was a happy one. He drifted into the darkness with the peaceful smile that they all have; that is, all except for me, who yet remains. A few years after that, I met Michael, one of Violetta's sons, born the year after I passed. He was a young man, handsome, and he told me tales of the second Great War that had sent him to the window-room. Michael lingered quite a while at his window, gazing at his siblings and at one particular auburn-haired young woman, before he moved on.

I am as restless here as I was on earth, busying myself whenever I can. I've become a sort of shepherd in the window-room. When new souls arrive, I show them to their windows, and then I vanish, like the gray-haired woman on the boat. I've thought perhaps I am cursed for what I did. Yet there is joy in bringing people to their windows for the first time, seeing their faces glow like lanterns in the dark as they keep their vigils.

Perhaps the Catholics got one thing right: confession is healthy for the soul. If this be my first Confession in one hundred years, it might also be my last, for I feel lighter of heart, fleeter of foot. I feel another sort of window has opened, through which, perhaps, I can be seen. I've seen my own half-Irish grandchildren, and I've learned how much the world has changed and will do so always. Perhaps it is time, after all, for me to go.

A brightness beckons me now. Do not forget me. Do not forget the kind of love that can break through the firmest boundaries and let in sound and light.

Shoe Tree by Warren Muzak

ARTICLE

The Wonder of "The Thing on the Fourble Board"
Denise Noe

Quiet, Please was a radio series that often aired episodes in the horror genre. It was created and written by Wyllis Cooper, also famous for creating similar radio series called *Lights Out*. On August 8, 1948, *Quiet, Please* aired "The Thing on the Fourble Board," an episode that is considered one of the greatest radio horror episodes ever and quite possibly one of the greatest ever regardless.

The episode starts in a deceptively mundane manner with a fellow talking to a guest. The folksy way he talks to the guest, coupled with the guest's silence throughout the episode, means that he sounds like is talking directly to the audience.

"Me, I'm a roughneck," he says. "At least, I was a roughneck, I mean twenty years. ago, a little too old, too slow now. Besides, I got a dollar now, don't have to be a roughneck. Married, got a nice home." He is soon calling: "Mike! Mike!" Then he informs us that his wife's name is Maxine but she prefers to be called Mike. Since "mike" is also short for microphone, the story is already playing with our expectations. The narrator must go aways from the "mike" to call "Mike." Then he lets us know she is probably in the kitchen — a usual place for a wife in the era and a not uncommon place in ours — and failed to answer his call because "she doesn't hear very well."

Our narrator details what he means by a "roughneck." That is someone who works on an oil field in a drilling crew. He tells us that it is not a job "for a guy with a bow tie." In other words, the fellows who work there are rough, tough, crude, beer-guzzling sorts. They are not intellectuals or philosophers or deep thinkers. Despite the usual characteristics of the roughnecks, the nature of the job leads to scientific curiosity: "I don't think there's an oil man in the world that don't wonder one time or another what's down there besides rock and oil and gas." He ruminates on the fact that they pull up oil made of "trees that died twenty million years ago" or "made of dinosaur bones," or perhaps even of the "flesh and blood of men that beat each other to death with a stone axe, ate saber tooth tiger for lunch." Indeed, the nature of the job is that a roughneck can't help but "get to wondering" when he sees "cores that come up from way down there" and are composed of such things as trilobites that lived when New York was buried under ice. Our narrator elaborates that he and another worker "found something once" and, perhaps more significantly, "something found us."

Then he explains that finding that "something" — and being found by it — is what this story is about.

This pivotal event that occurred some twenty years ago. Our narrator was on the oil drilling site when joined by geologist Billy Gruenwald. We now learn that the narrator's name is Porky — and has been cooking pork chops that he offers to share with Billy. Author Cooper is clearly having fun with this play on words. We hear the sizzling of cooking and the pair sit down to share pork chops. They discuss the drilling and the geologist observes that they are "getting into shale." Later he says we "never can tell what's down there." At one point, finding Billy inexplicably confused, Porky grumpily asks, "What's eating you?" Thus, another reference to eating is made. Billy says he thinks there is "somebody up there on that fourble board."

Ah, the title. What *is* a fourble board? Porky leaves the conversation with Billy to return to the present, explaining to silent guest and audience that "drill pipe comes in lengths" that are handled with "several lengths screwed together. Two lengths is a double, three is a treble, four is a fourble." The pipe is pulled up the derrick "with a traveling block which moves up and down from the crown block" at the derrick's top. Returning to the story, he recalls that nobody was on the fourble board save an owl that flew away.

The two men enjoy pork chops and booze as they chat. The issue of fears happens to come up and Billy sheepishly admits he's afraid of the dark. Confession begets confession and Porky tells him he fears spiders.

Soon Billy makes a startled cry. He shows Porky that he found an item embedded in a core they brought up. "It couldn't be!" Porky exclaims when he sees the item. Billy notes, "That rock there comes from a mile underground — and it's been a mile underground for a million years."

Porky sees that Billy holds "a gold ring" that is "carved and filigreed just like jewelry." Porky pokes at the rock core and finds what appears to be a finger made of stone." When Billy rubs mud off the stone finger, it is no longer visible but Billy says he still feels it and it makes a "clunk" when he drops it.

Shocked and confused, pair finish off a bottle of booze. Porky falls sleep. He dreams about black widow spiders with gold rings on their legs crawling on him. As he awakens, he believes he hears Billy climbing the ladder to the fourble board. When fully awake, Porky sees Billy lying dead on the floor, his neck broken. Apparently he has fallen from the fourble board. Porky recalls that Porky had put the mysterious ring on his left hand's little finger: both finger and ring are missing from the corpse.

Terrified, Porky runs outside and gets in Billy's car. But Porky has not got the key and cannot bring himself to return to the corpse to "go through a dead man's clothes." He shivers in the vehicle until the next morning when the crew, together with foreman Ted, arrive. They discover the body and Porky is taken to the police station. After intense questioning, Ted and the detective conducting the interrogation conclude there was no homicide but only an accident.

Ted convinces Porky to return to the worksite. When he does, another accident follows that kills Ted! After two fatal accidents so close together, the crew understandably quits. However, Porky cannot get his mind off the derrick worksite. He returns to investigate. He hears a "tinkle" of something hitting the ground and finds the gold ring that seemingly came from "a mile underground and from a million years ago in time."

Even more inexplicably, he hears "the sound of a kid crying." Although Porky describes them that way, the wails the audience hears are so bizarre sounding that we cannot definitely identify them as human. The wails increase in volume but Porky still sees nothing. He yells for anyone present to reveal themselves. Then he shoots in the direction of the bizarre sounds. There is neither verbal reply and nothing to be seen. The sounds that reminded him of a "kid crying" now remind him of the "meowing" of a cat. He spots a big can of red paint and throws it at the sound.

Then he sees "The Thing on the Fourble Board." It possesses the "face of a little girl." There is a finger missing from its left hand. The bulk of the body resembles that of a gigantic spider. He realizes, "It'd come from the bowels of the earth, come riding up on the drill pipe as we yanked it out of the well. Come to an alien world. And was lost." The creature, human-like on top and spider-like below, stood covered with red paint. It reached out to put it hand on Porky's arm and its hand was "stone. Living, moving stone." The Thing looked into Porky's eyes at it "mewed like a lost kitten."

Porky pulls us to the present when he says "Twenty years ago." In the two decades since he discovered the Thing, he has learned much about it. He has learned what it eats, that it does not hear well, that it is invisible and blind but becomes both visible and sighted if "sprayed with mud or paint or greasepaint" or just has makeup on it. He likes its "pathetic, little girl face" and finds it "beautiful" when well-made up." There is something very special about the process of "making it up, rubbing greasepaint on a stone face that looks at you and smiles and makes sounds like a lost kitten." He is offended by its body but can disguise it in long dresses. Perhaps most ominously, he says, "When she's hungry, I have to stay out of her way." He tells the silent guest to "sit still or I'll have to shoot you." Finally, he informs the guest, "I want you to meet my wife. Or, rather, my wife wants to meet you." Again he leans aways from the mic to call, "Mike?" There is the sound of a door opening and a kind of "clank clank" of heavy shoes.

Mike makes the same sort of noises we have previously heard. She is the Thing. And it appears that the guest — the audience — is her next meal!

Spider creature by Ben Garriga

At the end of the episode, we are told that Ernest Chappell played the starring role, as he usually did in *Quiet, Please*. Van Sutter played Billy and Pat O'Malley was Ted. The actor who played a police officer is not credited. But we are told, "Cecil Roy was also a member of the cast."

What makes this episode so special? Part of it is the oddity of the "marriage" between this subterranean creature to a human man. Although I have a vivid imagination, I find it hard to visualize how this marriage was consummated, given the limitations imposed by a spider-type body as well as those imposed by an upper body which, however human-like, is made of stone or similar material. However, it is possible to understand the emotional bond between Porky and Mike. Porky has a sense of responsibility toward this creature because he yanked out of her natural habitat and drew her into "an alien world." In his attraction to her, there is an odd element of daddy-dolling as he so enjoys looking at her "pathetic little girl face" as well as putting makeup on her.

Cecil Roy

Another factor that makes the episode magnificently creepy is Cecil Roy's vocal performance in making sounds that could not possibly be in any language yet convey emotions like fear and confusion. It was fitting that the show's makers cast actress Roy to give voice to the creature since she was called "The Girl with a Thousand Voices." Her vocal versatility made her an in-demand radio performer as she could believably voice an infant, toddler, teenager, a mature woman, or even elderly woman. This vocal virtuoso was able to assume at least twenty dialects. She was the voice of the title character in the animated cartoon *Little Lulu* series from 1944-1962 as well as the title character of the *Casper the Friendly Ghost* series in the 1940s-1950s.

Although superb crafting is vital to the effectiveness of "The Thing on the Fourble Board," this writer believes that the most important key to the power — to its creepiness — is that way it zeroes on intriguing natural mysteries In this way, it resembles another *Quiet, Please* episode, "Let the Lillies Consider", that I discussed in my essay "Radio Dramas On the Mystery of Plant 'Consciousness.'" In that piece, I noted that Cooper struck a responsive chord with the listening audience by building an episode around the tantalizing possibility that plants may experience emotions.

The mysteries that give "Fourble Board" its haunting quality have to do with what another mystery: What is inside the earth? Geologists have formed valid scientific ideas but they are inevitably engaging in a certain amount of guesswork. We have not been far down inside out planet so we cannot *know*. We can be certain that, contrary to some folklore, the earth is not hollow. But how can we know that there might not be large cavities under the surface? How can we know what species might have developed inside the world?

A creative melding of author insider jokes, subterranean fantasy, and auras of both bestiality and pedophilia make "The Thing on the Fourble Board" a uniquely eerie listening experience.

ARTICLE

Dying is Easy – Coming Back is Hard
Anonymous
As told to Alice Ward

This is a true recount of an actual personal experience. The name is omitted for privacy.

"We're about to put you to sleep," a calm, reassuring voice told me. "Relax—you'll feel a little sting at first as the medicine goes through your IV line. You'll wake up when it's all over. Do you have any questions?"

I looked up into the eyes of the anesthesiologist. "I'm a little scared. I've never had major surgery before, only stuff like tonsils."

"That's okay—it's normal to be nervous. Your surgery won't take long, and you'll be back in your room in time for lunch." The skin around his eyes crinkled as he smiled; his mouth was hidden by his surgical mask. "Your surgeon is going to repair the hernia. I'm sure he told you it's a matter of making sure the abdominal wall is strengthened. He's not even taking anything out."

"That's what he said," I agreed. "He also told me to take it easy this summer and save the strenuous activity for the fall semester."

"Got to give this time to heal. Think of it this way: you have an incision and he's fixing it. You're in college?"

"Just finished my first year of pre-med."

"Well, good luck with that. As far as this goes, I'll be with you every step."

"I'm in your hands," I murmured as I closed my eyes, "and His." A warm, burning sensation traveled up my arm into my chest.

I felt as if I was flying, lighter than air—and realized I was looking down at an operating table. It didn't bother me for some reason, even as I recognized that the body on the table was mine. An out-of-body experience was not new to me, although I had learned to keep the incidents to myself after one teacher regarded me as a psych case when I described it to her.

This was different. As I watched, the medical team began setting up equipment, and calling out orders to each other.

My perceptions changed. One instant I was in the operating room—the next I was floating in darkness. It felt friendly and welcoming, not at all frightening. I was still me, with no sense of having any defined body.

My senses expanded as if I had never used them. Everything was new. Lights flashed, but they had tastes. Sounds had colors. Colors had shapes. The darkness remained but took on new forms, each with heightened sensations. All the while, I felt enveloped in a peaceful tranquility, knowing I was safe. My mind—the essence of what I am—reached out for more of the experiences. Levels of stimulation which cannot be defined surrounded me, comforting me. I was home.

I had a vague impression of a negative, conveyed to me without words as a feeling from everywhere around me. *Not your time.*

Suddenly, I spiraled down and down into a vortex as if I had been floating in a warm bathtub and some huge hand had pulled the plug. I grew heavy as the light freedom dissipated abruptly and the friendly warmth turned into cold. As a metal tape measure is snapped back into its casing, I was in my body and all the wondrous sensations gone.

Pain. Cold. Every nerve in my being tingled, sending waves of shocks through me. I was lying on a hard surface, with something rhythmically pressing down on my chest. I wanted to protest, to stop them, that I had been fine where I had been, and I wanted to go back. I could not move. I lay there, totally exhausted, miserable, shivering, and unable to communicate. My hearing returned first.

"She's back," a voice I recognized the anesthesiologist's voice. It trembled.

"That was too close," my doctor responded with obvious relief. "What triggered this?"

"She may have an allergy to one of the anesthetics," he

replied. "I'll tell her when she waked up."

"She's very young," a nurse observed. "Will she remember anything?"

"Probably not, which might be for the best."

"Thank God."

When I did wake up, the anesthesiologist was sitting at my bedside, looking like he was dozing. He needed a shave. I cleared my throat, and he sat up straight.

"Welcome back," he said with a big grin.

I looked beyond him to see aides delivering lunch trays to other rooms.

"You said I'd be back in my room by lunch."

"I said that yesterday." He paused while I took that in."

"I was out for a whole day?" I was stunned.

"What do you remember?" he asked, with no response to my question.

"Not much. It's blurry. I think something kept pounding on my chest."

He smiled. "You would remember that. We used CPR on you."

"You're saying I *died* on the operating table?"

"You went into cardio-vascular shock and we almost lost you."

I thought about what he had said. "Before I went into surgery I asked you to make sure you didn't tell my mother if something went wrong," I reminded him.

"You're legally an adult, so we told her we were holding you for observation before returning you to your room. She's coming later this afternoon."

"You told me you would stay with me. Thank you." I finally asked the big question. "What did go wrong?"

"Make sure no one ever uses sodium pentothal as an anesthetic agent for you," he instructed me. "Tell them you're allergic to it. I don't want anyone else to have to go through this."

I did not try to explain what I had experienced to him, or anyone else for a long time. Some of it dimmed immediately after the incident, only to return later. The outcome is simple: I survived.

The experience changed me, of course. I lost my sense of elapsing time, so I wear a watch, which is no big deal. A few minor things shifted a bit—my sense of direction got lost. Literally.

The deep change, the major one, was in sensitivity. I had always been sensitive to the emotions of those around me. I could pick up on feelings as easily as picking up a coffee cup. It was years before I came to recognize and master the empathic talent I now possess, which I recognize as the biggest change. Empathy is a sharp-edged tool; it can cut both ways. Control is essential and I had to learn the ins and outs on my own as I matured.

We all have our time. I have never attempted to put the experience into words before, mainly because there is no way to accurately recount what I experienced. When asked about it, I always quip, "Dying is easy—coming back is hard."

www.ingramcontent.com/pod-product-compliance
Lightning Source LLC
LaVergne TN
LVHW012027060526
838201LV00061B/4495